"Okay, I'll prove it to you,"

Amy told Jake as she handed him the book.

"*This* proves that you have to get married before you're twenty-five?"

"It showed me all the pitfalls a woman faces. The biggest problem is the shortage of men. And a lot of available men will never settle down."

"So what? I'm not married and I've never minded," Jake retorted.

"That's *exactly* my point! But I do want to get married." Amy's tone was wistful. "Having a family is important to me. I want kids and someone to share my life with. Is that so terrible?"

"Of course not," Jake said, clearing his throat. "And I'll do what I can to help."

As the words left his mouth, a look of horror filled his face. "Wait a minute," he said as he jumped up, knocking over his chair.

"You aren't planning on marrying *me,* are you?" he demanded hoarsely.

Dear Reader,

August is vacation month, and no matter where you're planning to go, don't forget to take along this month's Silhouette Romance novels. They're the perfect summertime read! And even if you can't get away, you can still escape from it all for a few hours of love and adventure with Silhouette Romance books.

August continues our WRITTEN IN THE STARS series. Each month in 1992 we're proud to present a book that focuses on the hero and his astrological sign. This month we're featuring the proud, passionate Leo man in Suzanne Carey's intensely emotional *Baby Swap*.

You won't want to miss the rest of our fabulous August lineup. We have love stories by Elizabeth August, Brittany Young, Carol Grace and Carla Cassidy. As a special treat, we're introducing a talented newcomer, Sandra Paul. And in months to come, watch for Silhouette Romance novels by many more of your favorite authors, including Diana Palmer, Annette Broadrick and Marie Ferrarella.

The Silhouette Romance authors and editors love to hear from readers and we'd love to hear from *you*.

Happy reading from all of us at Silhouette!

Valerie Susan Hayward
Senior Editor

SANDRA PAUL

Last Chance for Marriage

Silhouette *Romance*

Published by Silhouette Books New York

America's Publisher of Contemporary Romance

For my parents, Janet and Virgil,
who believed in me before I did.
Thank you for all your encouragement and support.

And for my husband, Paul, my "Mr. Right."

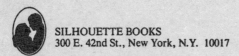

SILHOUETTE BOOKS
300 E. 42nd St., New York, N.Y. 10017

LAST CHANCE FOR MARRIAGE

ISBN: 0-373-08883-3

First Silhouette Books printing August 1992

Printed in the U.S.A.

SANDRA PAUL

married her high school sweetheart and they live in Southern California with their three children, two dogs and a cat.

For years, she did housework with a book in one hand until friends at Sunshine Books in Buena Park told her about Romance Writers of America. She joined RWA and began writing, but soon discovered writing, reading *and* housework were too much to handle. She gave up housework.

Last Chance for Marriage, the winner of an RWA Golden Heart Award, is her first book.

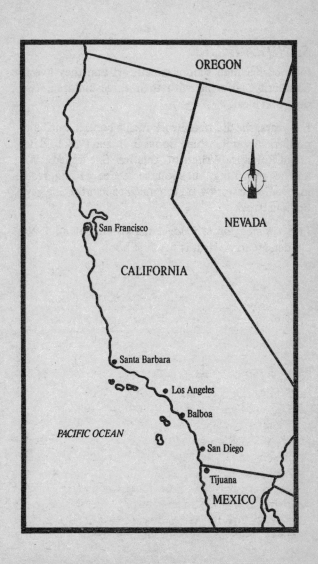

Chapter One

"Amy can't stay here!"

"Why not?"

"I'll tell you why not! Because she's a pain in the..."

"Jake Joseph Weston! Just because you and Amy sometimes disagree—" Jake snorted at his grandmother's understatement and switched the phone to his other ear "—doesn't mean you can't get along for a little while. Her lease on her new apartment begins the first of September."

"That's two months away! Look, Maddie, I'm swamped at work and I'd have no time to do any entertaining. She'd be bored stiff." Tucking the receiver between his shoulder and jaw, Jake pulled open the refrigerator: two cans of beer, assorted bottles of salad dressing and one shriveled peach. He slammed the door shut. "Why does she want to come to Balboa, anyway? Isn't she teaching summer school?"

"All the home ec classes were snatched up by teachers with more seniority."

"Can't she stay at your house while you're on your cruise?"

"She would, except the interior decorator I've hired is scheduled to start remodeling as soon as I leave next week."

Madelyn had her excuses down pat; too pat, Jake decided suspiciously. "How come you're so anxious to have her stay here? You wouldn't be trying a little matchmaking, would you, Maddie?" He opened the refrigerator again and took out the peach. Turning it to the least-shriveled side, he bit experimentally, carefully avoiding a large brown spot.

Madelyn laughed lightly. "Matchmaking? Between you and Amy? Darling, give me credit for some common sense. If something was going to develop between you two it would have happened long before now. Let her stay, dear, you have plenty of room. After all," she said, her voice dropping to quaver convincingly, "she helped me when I needed it."

Jake threw away the half-eaten peach. Leaning back against the kitchen door frame, he rubbed the tense muscles in his neck. He'd lived with Madelyn Weston from the time he was sixteen until he finished college at twenty-three. She might be a lady in every sense of the word; she might be seventy-five years old. Neither fact stopped her from hitting below the belt when she felt it was necessary. Emotional blackmail was her specialty.

He answered with strained patience. "Maddie, if you're referring—again—to the time you broke your arm, you know you refused to come here and I couldn't stay in Santa Barbara any longer. I was—"

"Busy at work," Madelyn finished, "as usual."

"I had three houses underway. I thought you understood."

"I did understand."

"Yeah? Then why throw it in my face constantly?"

Her tones swelled with hurt dignity. "I'm doing no such thing. I realize that at thirty you have your own life to lead. Far be it from me to complain because my only grandson—my only living relative—is so involved in his business he can only visit his grandmother a few times a year."

"Thank you for not complaining, Maddie."

"I'm just grateful Amy came to stay. She's been so much help these past two years, sometimes I forget she isn't my own flesh and blood. She's *such* a sweet girl."

"Yeah, a real saint." He shook his head in disbelief when Maddie, taking his words at face value, launched into a running monologue on Amy's virtues. Sighing, Jake pulled an oak chair closer and sat down, knowing from experience she wouldn't be winding down anytime soon.

It wasn't that he didn't like Amy. He did. *Sometimes.* And he owed her a lot. If it wasn't for her, he would have been forced to sell his business in Balboa to take care of Maddie when she'd adamantly refused to come to his beach house which had once belonged to her and his grandfather. "I'm more lonely for your grandfather there," Maddie had said when Jake tried to persuade her.

He'd been relieved, but not surprised, when Amy volunteered to stay with his grandmother. From the day Amy's father moved in next door to Maddie more than ten years ago, the lonely teenager and the older woman were firm friends. When Mr. Larkin remarried and moved out of state a couple of years ago, Amy opted to remain in Santa Barbara. From then on, Jake's visits to his grandmother ''coincidentally'' coincided with Amy's visits to her father, thus ensuring Maddie was never alone.

Yeah, no one, Jake thought as he idly knocked chunks of mud off his work boots onto the hardwood floor, was more soft-hearted than Amy about those she cared for. But soft-hearted or not, a saint Amy wasn't. Maddie saw her as a sweet young lady; Jake knew her better as a snub-nosed, blue-eyed tomboy with her brown hair in a ponytail and trouble up her sweatshirt sleeve.

Trouble for him, that is. Like the time she was fifteen and she followed him around, taking notes in a thick black notebook. ''I'm documenting you,'' she'd told him when he confronted her one day in Maddie's living room. ''Like they do chimpanzees in the wild.'' He'd been wild, all right. Wild enough to shake the living daylights out of her if she hadn't darted behind Maddie for protection.

Or there was the time when she persuaded him to try a sugar-free apple pie she'd made. Unsuspectingly, he had wolfed the pie down and later discovered the sugar substitute she'd used was a natural laxative. Okay, maybe she hadn't done it on purpose and maybe he could look back on both incidents now and smile. The bottom line was that, all too often, Amy caused his gut to churn with frustration. And right now, with his contracting business taking off, he didn't have time for an emotional bellyache.

Convincing Madelyn, however, was another story. As she rattled on, his gaze absently roamed the room, sharpening abruptly at the sight of a black banana buried beneath a pile of dishes on the opposite counter. "Big help"..."no trouble"..."darling girl"...crackled into the air as he stretched the phone cord to investigate. Pulling back the banana's limp peel, he groaned. Black all the way through, darn it.

Disappointed, he returned the receiver to his ear. "...and at least she'll inspire you to get your place in order. I'm sure it's a pigsty," Madelyn concluded on a deep breath.

Jake looked with rueful respect at the phone in his hand. How did she know these things?

"Can she stay?" Maddie persisted.

Jake opened his mouth to say no. Amy would disrupt his life. He'd bet on it.

"As a favor to me?" his grandmother added quietly.

Yeah, Maddie knew how to fight dirty. "Send her down next week," he said, acknowledging defeat.

"Thank you, dear. I'm sure you two will have a wonderful visit." Madelyn paused. "Oh, and one more thing..."

Jake stiffened. *Here it comes.*

"If Amy needs your help..." she continued.

"What!"

"I'm not saying she will, dear, just that she might. She has an interesting little plan in mind. She's *so* creative!"

"She's a pain in the—"

"Goodbye, dear."

The phone clicked in his ear, and resignedly Jake slammed his receiver down, too. He stood, stretched and opened a cupboard by his head, brightening at the sight of a dusty red box in the corner. Did bouillon cubes go stale? he wondered.

* * *

A week later, Amy sat at Jake's kitchen table holding a chipped mug. She gently swirled the cup, watching as darker specks in the muddy liquid sank repeatedly to the bottom while pieces of green onion floated stubbornly at the top. She looked at Jake, seated across from her.

"You made this yourself?" she asked.

He nodded. "Yeah. I knew after your drive down this morning, you'd want something warm and soothing."

He was right, Amy decided. She did want something warm and soothing. She also wanted a hot bath, the chance to change out of her grubby gray sweat suit, and a long nap.

What she didn't want was whatever he had concocted in this mug.

She slowly lifted the cup to her lips. Steam—smelling faintly of, was it chicken?—tickled her nose. She took a sip, swallowed warm salty water and a piece of onion, and forced a smile. Her students had made worse, she told herself bracingly. If she took tiny sips she might be able to drink the whole thing.

After all, Jake was doing his best to welcome her. He'd made the mystery drink, he'd stayed home on a workday, and the brief tour he'd given her of the wood-framed, two-story bungalow showed he'd cleaned up. The living room was dusted and his downstairs bedroom straightened. In the guest bedroom upstairs he'd piled sheets, yellowed with age but fresh, on the tarnished brass bed. The kitchen was only slightly cluttered, and the one bathroom, a converted pantry boasting a blue, claw-footed bathtub, reeked of disinfectant.

Yes, Jake was doing his best to make her comfortable. More importantly, he obviously had the housework under control.

Which meant, Amy decided as she took another sip, that Madelyn Weston had a lot to answer for. Maddie might be the kindest person Amy had ever met; she might be as honest as the day was long. Neither fact stopped her from bending the truth when she felt it was necessary. Avoiding the issue was her specialty.

"Jake needs *my* help keeping house this summer?" Amy had asked the older woman days ago as they packed for Maddie's cruise. "You're *positive* he didn't invite me to stay because he feels obligated or pressured because I've been staying with you?"

"Darling, he's thrilled to have you visit." Catching sight of Amy's skeptical expression, Madelyn had amended, "Well, maybe not thrilled, but certainly happy."

"He said he was 'happy' about it?"

Madelyn's voice was muffled as her tall figure, draped in a vibrant blue-and-green silk kimono, burrowed through the rainbow of clothes in her closet. "Maybe not those exact words, dear. You know Jake."

Amy's skepticism deepened. Yes, she did know Jake. And not once during the past ten years had he ever looked happy to see her. Resigned? Yes. Happy? No.

"You did tell him my plans for the summer, didn't you, Maddie?" Amy persisted, trying to catch her gaze. "About how I'm changing my 'school teacher' image and looking for a husband?"

"I think I mentioned something about it, darling," Madelyn answered vaguely. "Even if I didn't, Jake is sure to notice you've slimmed down."

Amy raised a disbelieving eyebrow. "Jake? Notice I've changed? He still sees me as a bumbling teenager." She refolded a velvet skirt Maddie had stuffed into the case and laid it neatly on the growing pile of clothes. "Besides, I don't care if he notices. I do care if, from some misguided protectiveness, he interferes with my plans."

Madelyn's silver-gray eyes widened in surprise. "Darling, Jake would never interfere. He'll probably help."

Amy paused in her packing to consider the novel idea. "Jake? Do you really think so? It *would* make it easier to meet men."

"Of course he will, dear," Maddie said firmly. "He's changed. He's *very* easygoing now."

Thinking about Maddie's last remark, Amy grimaced. Maddie's wrong, she thought. Jake never changes except to grow browner and tougher. Looking over the rim of her cup, she studied the man opposite. His skin was a smooth golden brown, accentuating the darker chestnut of his lashes, brows, and the crisp curls on his head. Years of working in the sun had etched tiny lines at the corners of his teasing gray eyes. His nose was bluntly masculine, his mouth cleanly cut.

Beneath his red plaid shirt, the powerful muscles in his neck, shoulders and arms were sculpted into rock-hard curves by almost a decade of manual labor. He was just under six feet tall, but his lean hips and broad shoulders gave an illusion of greater height.

Characteristically, his lean jaw jutted forward unrelentingly as it had ever since Amy mentioned paying rent a little earlier. The words were barely out of her mouth before he cut her off. The discussion, he stated firmly, was closed. Amy was a guest and guests did not pay rent.

He's easygoing, all right, she thought wryly. As easygoing as a brick wall. However, one thing she had learned while living with Maddie was: you don't go through brick walls, you go around them. Whether Jake liked it or not, this guest would earn her keep, possibly by helping with the housework and the cooking. She took another sip of her salty drink. Hopefully, all the cooking.

"Do you like it?"

Jolted from her thoughts by Jake's deep voice, Amy stared at him blankly. "What?"

"Do you like the drink? I made it with bouillon cubes."

"Oh." Bouillon? Amy looked down at her cup. Empty, thank goodness. "It was…interesting. The onions were a nice touch." She put the cup down. It was time to tackle another issue, and she might as well get it over with. "Jake, I have a problem."

His silver-gray eyes, so like his grandmother's, fastened on her intently. "What problem?"

"In two months, on September 1, I'm going to be twenty-five years old."

Jake raised a questioning brow. What was the big deal? She looked more like seventeen than twenty-four, anyway. Partly because she was such a shorty, only about five one, and partly because her brown hair was escaping the bun she'd secured it in. It tumbled around her pale face in a curly mass. Her bare pink mouth didn't have a hint of a smile, and her blue eyes looked anxious as she met his gaze. "So?"

Amy leaned forward. "So, by the time women reach twenty-five, they outnumber single men by over seven million!" Having dropped her bomb, she slouched back and waited for Jake's reaction.

"So?"

"Jake! Don't you see? I'm going to be an outnumbered single woman! How will I—a home ec teacher at a small junior high school—ever find someone to marry? There are only four men at the school where I work. One is the custodian and he's at least sixty-five. Two of them, the boys' coach and the wood-shop teacher, are already married, and the last one is the principal, who must weigh over three hundred pounds. And he's a rude, overbearing man whom I wouldn't marry if you paid me."

"The fat principal wants to marry you?" he asked, hiding a grin.

"No, he doesn't want to marry me! I just mean I wouldn't marry him even if he did."

"Now, let me get this straight." He sat forward in his chair. She surely wasn't serious about all this. Was she? "You're going to be twenty-five in three months—"

"Two months."

"In two months. Right?"

Amy nodded. "Right."

"And you're afraid if you don't get married before then you never will. Right?"

"Right."

Jake stood up and went to refill his cup as Amy watched anxiously. Turning, he leaned his hips against the oak counter. "Well, Amy, I can see you certainly do have a problem." He took another sip of his bouillon drink.

Amy breathed a sigh of relief. "I knew you'd understand."

"Oh, I understand all right. The problem is—you're crazy."

"Jake!"

"Oh, come on, Amy," he said in exasperation. "You can't believe that unless you get married by twenty-five, you never will."

"It's true." The expression on his face didn't change. Amy stood up determinedly and grabbed her straw purse from a nearby chair. "Okay, I'll prove it to you." Slamming the large bag on the counter near Jake, she pulled out a book and thrust it into his hands. "Here. Read this."

Juggling the book in one hand, Jake set his cup down and turned the book over. A pretty blond woman beamed at him from the front cover. *"How to Find Your Perfect Mate.* This? This is your proof? A book by Joan Potocki?"

"Dr. Joan Potocki."

"Well, excuse me. *Dr.* Joan Potocki. What does this have to do with anything?"

Amy tapped the book significantly. "In this book I learned all the pitfalls a woman faces when looking for a husband in the nineties. The biggest problem is the shortage of men."

"What a bunch of bull."

"It is not! Listen to this." Amy grabbed the book away and began reading. "According to the last census, there are over seven million more single women than men in the United States. This is primarily because of the higher death rate among males. In fact, by age twenty-five, there are already more women than men.''

Pausing, Amy lowered her voice and added, "From then on it's a losing battle." She slammed the book shut.

"Oh, my God!"

"Jake, you can't argue with facts. And the short-age of men isn't the only problem. What with the pill, religious calling—whatever—the leftover single men sometimes don't want to get married.''

"Okay, okay." She *was* serious about all this stuff. Studying her intent face, Jake raked his fingers through his hair. "Supposing what the book says is true. So what? I'm not married and I've never minded.''

"That's *exactly* my point!''

"But there must be thousands, probably millions, of women who don't want to get married, either.''

"Maybe there are. But I do want to. Having a fam-ily is important to me." Turning away, she sat down at the table. She traced the grain running through the wood, avoiding his gaze. "For one thing, I want kids, and I believe children need two parents. Also, I want someone to share my life with, someone I'm compat-ible with." She sent Jake a fleeting glance and dropped her eyes again. "I've only told Maddie this, but Mom and Dad didn't get along. He almost seemed relieved when she died, and, well, he and I have never been close, either, no matter how I try. I know they say you can't miss what you've never had, but believe me, I've missed not having a family.''

For a moment she pressed her lips firmly together and clasped her hands in her lap. Then, looking up at him, she smiled faintly and added, "I like people,

Jake. That's why I was so glad to have Maddie living next door. I pretended she was the grandmother I didn't have. And when you came to visit her... well, sometimes I pretended you were my family, too." A slight flush rose in her pale cheeks.

Jake frowned. He knew Amy had lost her mother when she was fourteen. He'd been sixteen when both his parents had died in a car crash. Between him and Amy, though, Jake decided he'd been the luckier. He'd had Maddie. In his opinion, Amy's father was straitlaced and cold, unable to respond to Amy's impulsive warmth. The hugs and kisses dispersed so freely by Madelyn on a grieving and sometimes withdrawn grandson had been non-existent in the Larkin household.

Jake swung his chair backward, straddling it as he sat down next to her. Reaching out, he covered her smooth hand with his callused one. "I think of you as family, too, Amy."

She turned her hand upward to clasp his much larger one. "Thanks, Jake."

His eyebrows drew together as he frowned. "But isn't it kind of *calculating* to hunt for a husband?"

"I'm not being calculating." Releasing his hand, Amy straightened. "All I'm trying to do is increase the odds that something wonderful will happen. By looking for a man with my head instead of just my emotions, maybe I can avoid some of the heartache my father and mother went through." Her gaze searched his tanned face. "Is that so terrible?"

Jake met her eyes. "Of course it's not." Amy smiled tremulously at him, and he cleared his throat, adding, "And I'll do what I can to help."

As the words left his mouth a look of dawning horror filled his face. "Oh, my God!" He jumped up, knocking over his chair.

"Jake! What is it?"

"You aren't planning on marrying *me* are you?" he demanded hoarsely.

Chapter Two

Amy stared at him uncomprehendingly for a moment before her face crumpled into laughter.

"Marry you? Jake," she said, crossing her arms and holding her sides, "please . . . give me a break."

Jake lifted the chair from the floor and set it upright. She'd done it again. She'd made him feel warm inside, and then—WHAM!—she hit him with a sucker punch. He could feel his gut tightening into a familiar painful knot.

Unlike most women he knew, Amy laughed unrestrainedly. Her blue eyes danced, her soft mouth widened in an attractive grin, and her breathless chuckles were usually infectious. Not this time. He didn't have the least inclination even to smile. For one thing, her reaction made him feel like an egotistical fool. More importantly, for some crazy reason, he also felt a little hurt. *Some* women considered him attractive. *They* certainly didn't howl with laughter at the thought of marrying him.

He waited until her laughter had subsided into an occasional chuckle. "It's not that funny, you know."

Amy stifled a giggle. "Oh, I know. It's just your expression." She bugged her eyes and mimicked his low tones, "You aren't planning on marrying *me,* are you?" Catching sight of his expression, she stopped. "I mean, well, I've known you forever, Jake."

He grimaced. "Yeah, it does seem like forever. If you aren't planning on marrying me, for which we are *both* deeply thankful," he added emphatically, "then I don't see how I can help you." He crossed his sinewy arms in front of his chest and waited.

"Think about it, Jake." Amy stood up and began clearing the table. "You're a carpenter—"

"I'm a *contractor.*"

She brushed that aside. "Carpenter, contractor. For our purposes, they're all the same thing. The point is you have your own business."

"So?"

Amy carried the cups to the sink, and Jake stepped out of her way. "You have friends and a lot of men working for you. Correct?" She squirted in dish soap and plunged her hands into the soapy water.

"And?"

"And," Amy said, scrubbing at a mug, "some of the men are single. Right?" She glanced at Jake over her shoulder.

His eyes met hers and his square jaw tightened. "Now, just one minute, Amy. If you think you're going to cause chaos among my workers, you can think again. I have a big project going, and no way on God's green earth am I going to let you mess it up."

"I won't mess it up. For goodness' sake, I'm not planning on hanging around your job site." Turning, she waved a sudsy hand for emphasis. "All I'm asking is for you to…discreetly…introduce me to a nice single man."

Jake lifted a dark brow. "Only one?"

"Maybe two. Out of two, I figure one should like me enough to ask me out."

Jake's other brow rose.

"Okay, three. Three at the most. And there's no need for you to look so skeptical. I'm planning on buying new clothes, getting my hair trimmed. The works. If you'd bother to notice, I've already lost weight."

His eyes dropped to her chest. He said dryly, "Oh, I've noticed."

Her cheeks burning, Amy took her wet hands out of the sink and crossed her arms protectively across her breasts. Trust Jake to notice the weight had come off the wrong place.

She frowned at him. His grin only widened. "Will you stop teasing me and listen to what I'm saying?" Her tone became cajoling. "I'm not asking for much. Help me meet three nice single men." Her slim brown eyebrows lifted, and she added loftily, "It shouldn't be too hard since I don't judge a man on looks alone. Tall, dark and handsome is overrated in my opinion. I just want to meet someone who's nice."

"I see." With a gleam in his eyes, Jake rubbed his jaw. "All I have to do is find three nice, ugly, little guys for you. Preferably blondes."

She wrinkled her nose. "Very funny. But while we're on the subject, I have something to help you find the kind of man I want." Running her wet hands down the sides of her sweatpants, Amy walked over to her purse and began burrowing.

"Wait a minute, Amy. I haven't said I'd do it." Intent on her search, she ignored him. Resignedly, he asked, "What are you looking for now? Another book?"

"No," Amy answered. "A list."

"A list? A list of what?"

"A list of my requirements for a prospective husband, of course. The book recommended writing them out to visualize them better." Her hand closed on a rumpled sheet of notebook paper. "Here it is!" She pulled it out and waved it triumphantly.

"I don't need a list!"

Amy widened her eyes. "Are you telling me you know what to look for in a husband?"

"Sure. Well, no. Oh, give me the damn thing." He reached for the paper but she pulled it back out of reach.

"Now, these are *general* guidelines. I trust your judgment when it comes to making a final choice." She proffered the list a second time, and again yanked it away as another thought occurred to her. "Remember," she said quickly as Jake, losing patience, grasped her wrist to hold her hand still, "they don't have to fulfill every requirement."

"Fine." Jake twitched the paper out of her fingers. Dropping her wrist, he pulled a worn brown wallet out of his hip pocket, folded the paper and slipped it inside. He shoved the wallet back into his jeans. "I want you to pay attention now. I have a requirement for *you* to follow." He lifted her chin with his finger until her questioning blue eyes met his. "I'll think about bringing a couple of the guys over. But you are not—I repeat, *not*—to go overboard about this.''

He shook his head reproachfully as she began to protest. "I'm not going to argue about this, Amy. I don't want you doing something you might regret. There are some strange guys in this town, and the one smart thing you've done is to come to me. You're too impulsive on your own." He released her chin. "Now, I've got to get to work."

With Amy at his heels, he strode into the front room.

"I'm twenty-four, not fourteen, Jake Weston! I asked for your *help* in meeting some eligible men, but I certainly don't need your approval for anything I decide to do. And I am not impulsive!" she said to his broad back.

"Sure you're not. Maybe compulsive would be a better word." He lifted his leather jacket off the hook by the front door.

"When have I ever been compulsive?"

"Look at you now. You read a book, get an idea and go after a man full-speed ahead."

"We've already discussed my reasons, Jake."

"Fine. Here's another example. What about college?"

"What about it?"

"You became a fanatic about college," Jake said, slipping his arms into his jacket sleeves. "You not only finished high school a year early, you crammed four years of college into three. All you thought about was graduating early. You lost contact with most of your friends. You didn't date, which is why you're in this fix now. You were obsessed."

Amy put her hands on her hips. "That's not true. A lot of people don't have time to date when they're in college!"

"Oh, right. College students are notorious for being celibate." Facing her, he mirrored her stance. "Here's another one. A classic example of an Amy compulsion: what about that stupid egg you carried around for three weeks?"

Exasperated, Amy said, "I had to carry Hector around. It was a required project for my psychology class."

"Well, you didn't have to dress it up, did you? A stupid egg wearing a blue knitted hat."

"It was supposed to be my child, for goodness' sake! I couldn't leave it naked. And just because it annoyed you, you didn't have to kill it!" Amy jabbed lightly at Jake's chest.

His eyes narrowed. "That's just what I'm talking about! You become obsessed. It was an egg! A common, ordinary, chicken egg! And I didn't kill it. I accidentally sat on it when *you* left it on Maddie's couch!"

"I didn't leave it. He was napping." Caught up in the argument, her own eyes narrowed. "And I've always suspected you sat on him on purpose. You flatly told me you thought the whole experiment was crazy, and every time my poor lab partner came over, you stood around flexing and cracking your knuckles. You scared the guy witless!"

"He *was* witless, I had nothing to do with it. I still say the whole assignment was asinine. Any professor who pairs up first-year college students, pretends to marry them, and then tops it off by giving them an egg to baby-sit for a week, is off his rocker." He shook his head in disgust. "And the guy you got was a twerp."

"He was not a twerp." Amy leaned forward angrily. "Charles was always a perfect gentleman. He never tried a thing with me."

Jake shrugged. "So he was a smart twerp."

"Oh! Why don't you just admit you squashed Hector on purpose?"

Jake smiled grimly. "Believe me, Amy. No one sits on a rotten egg on purpose."

"He wasn't rotten!"

Jake opened the door and stepped outside into the chilly early-morning air. With his hand on the doorknob, he put his face close to hers. "It's time you learned to face facts." Enunciating each syllable slowly and distinctly, he said, "Hector was a bad egg."

The door closed firmly in Amy's face.

Four hours later, Jake hefted his hammer, letting it glide along his callused palm as he slammed it downward. A final nail shot cleanly into the plywood, anchoring it irrevocably to the ceiling beams. He rose from a crouch to his feet. In spite of his heavy work boots, he balanced easily on the roof of the newly erected house frame.

Only a hundred yards away, the ocean lapped gently at the sand. A stray breeze flowed over him, cooling the patches of perspiration that glued his shirt to his broad chest and back. He secured the hammer in the leather nail bag strapped around his hips, and tugged the shirt over his head. He ran it across his damp face, neck and under his arms before tossing it off the third-story roof.

Laughter, interspersed with pithy protests, wafted up. Jake walked to the edge of the sheeting, glanced down and grinned. The shirt had landed on the gray head of John Harris, his foreman, who peeled the shirt off and shook a threatening fist up at him before returning to the western novel he was reading as he ate his sack lunch.

Other members of the crew lounged in the shade nearby. Shorty, apparently abandoning his attempt to lose twenty pounds, munched a cupcake and traded an occasional joking insult with Gallarza and Mendez as they heated foil-wrapped burritos on the engine block of Hernando's black truck. Rod Waring, at twenty-five the youngest in Jake's crew, was the only member taking advantage of the unseasonably hot weather as he lay stretched out on the sand in the sun. Deeply tanned, with sun-bleached blond hair, he blended perfectly with the surfers lounging nearby. Only his low-riding denim jeans distinguished him from the others.

Jake sniffed appreciatively as the spicy smell of chicken burritos rose above the scent of salt air and newly cut pine. Gallarza's wife, Theresa, had a soft spot for "the poor, bachelor boss" and usually slipped in an extra burrito for him, but Jake decided not to go down yet. He wanted to be alone when he read Amy's list.

Thinking of her, he turned and looked out over the houses huddled together along the Balboa strip. His small bungalow was only eight blocks away, hidden in the mass of larger homes vying with one another for the best sea view. What was she doing now? He smiled. At least he'd gotten in the last word—with Amy, that was saying a lot.

The smile faded slowly. This morning she'd taken him by surprise. Somehow, probably because of the difference in their ages, he'd never thought about Amy as a woman, with all a woman's natural needs and desires. Hell, he still had a hard time realizing she'd been a certified teacher for two years! How had time gone by so fast? And how did the once-troublesome teenager who'd always seemed to be hanging around his grandmother's house keep a class of students, her size or larger, in line? Never mind teaching them anything.

Yet thinking of her teaching was easier than trying to imagine Amy married. After all, she'd been enthusiastically intent about studying, determined to get her degree quickly. He now suspected her urgency had something to do with wanting to be independent of her father as soon as possible. Why, Amy had spent every Christmas Eve for the past ten years with his grandmother. She'd fit in so naturally, he'd never considered that it was strange she wasn't with her father. He'd only been thankful his grandmother had young company close by, especially since his business had always demanded so much attention.

He stared out at the surfers rising and falling on the curling waves. But why this sudden desire to get married, he wondered? She'd admitted just this morning that he and Madelyn were almost like family. What more did she need? It was that stupid book. Find a mate by following a self-help book. Sure. But if trying made her feel better, what was the harm?

He walked slowly to the other side of the sheeting, then sat down and leaned his bare back against the slanted, sun-warmed wood. Squinting a little in the bright sunlight, he carefully unfolded the wrinkled paper. The first sentence, written in Amy's precise, feminine handwriting, jumped up at him.

Age: twenty-one to twenty-nine.

Jake sat up a little, his indulgent mood vanishing. Twenty-one? What did she want, a child? And what was so magic about age twenty-nine? Surely Amy didn't believe that garbage about a man being past his prime by thirty. Why, he could name at least three guys—four, including himself—who were in better shape at thirty than they'd ever been.

His brows knit slightly as his eyes moved to the next line. *A good sense of humor.* Fine. Great. A sense of humor, now that he could understand. A sense of humor was definitely important. As long as she didn't end up with some clown who didn't know when to take things seriously.

He snorted out loud as he read her next requirement. *A man who is neat and orderly, willing to do his part to make a home a pleasant place to be.* If Amy thought neatness was what made a person pleasant, she should try living with an old army sergeant.

Likes children. Jake shifted uncomfortably. She certainly was serious about kids. The image of Amy with a rounded belly drifted through his mind, and his stomach muscles clenched.

His eyes quickly moved to the last item on the list. *A liberated man who's sensitive, nonviolent and never domineering.* Definitely. Now she was on track. A man needed to be sensitive to a woman's feelings, especially a woman like Amy who kept so much bottled up inside.

Violence, of course, was never an answer. As for domineering . . . Jake unconsciously flexed his powerful biceps...well, he would personally rearrange the face of any guy who ever tried to dominate Amy.

On this positive thought, he stood up. A power saw whined to life below, and the boards beneath his feet vibrated as the men began hanging dry wall.

The breeze, brisker now, tugged at Amy's list. Carefully, Jake refolded it and tucked it back in his wallet. Well, he'd help her find a prospective husband. She could be irritating; hell, she could be downright infuriating, but he owed her a lot for all she'd done for Maddie. Amy, more than anyone he knew, certainly deserved the best.

And the sooner he found "Mr. Right," the sooner Amy's disruptive presence would be out of his life.

Chapter Three

"**I** want the best," Amy told the lady at the counter.

Ten minutes later, swathed in a turquoise plastic robe with the words The Cutting Edge emblazoned in orange across the front, Amy admitted to herself that maybe Jake was right. Maybe, just maybe, she was...a tad...impulsive. Who else but an impulsive idiot would march into the first hair salon she saw and ask for "the best"? During the past week, as she'd studied Dr. Potocki's book and busied herself getting Jake's house in order, she'd imagined being transformed by a stylist who'd exclaim over her good points; boost her self-esteem. In her mind, she'd pictured a kind-faced woman discussing with her the best way to proceed.

Reality was Harvey.

The slender blond man grasped Amy's chin firmly and turned it to the side. It wasn't only Harvey that was making her uncomfortable, Amy decided. The robe bothered her, too. Whenever she wore a robe that tied in the back—at the dentist's, the doctor's, or in hair salons—pain or humiliation followed. She hated pain and wasn't crazy about humiliation. She suspected Harvey specialized in both. If Jake hadn't assured her continuously that he already had someone in mind for her first date, she'd get up right now and walk out.

She lifted a hand to brush hair out of her eyes. Harvey gave her a disapproving glare, and she meekly lowered it again beneath the robe. Okay, maybe she wouldn't walk out. If Jake set her up with Prince Charming, she preferred to look like Cinderella, rather than one of the ugly stepsisters. And Harvey was the closest she'd come to finding a fairy godmother.

She tilted her head forward as he pulled two strands together under her chin. Harvey frowned at the hair he held. "Ah, ha! I thought so." He released her hair and circled to view her head from another angle. "One side of your hair is longer than the other. Where on earth did you get this cut?" He waited expectantly for her answer.

Amy could feel her cheeks begin to burn. "I cut it myself."

"You cut it yourself?" His eyes bulged. "What did you use? A dull knife?"

"Of course not. I used my manicure scissors..." Her voice trailed off as an expression of pain crossed the man's aristocratic features and he motioned for silence.

He thrust his hand through her hair, pushing her head this way and that. "Wrong. All wrong." Scooping up her hair again, he piled it on top of her head, holding it in place as he gauged the effect in the mirror. Nodding approvingly, he declared, "You need height. Lots of height! You are much too short." He swept the hair higher, revealing her small, pink ears.

"What you need—" Distracted by his own reflection, he dropped her hair, reaching up to delicately pull forward a golden curl onto the center of his high forehead. Expertly, he recombed the rest of his smooth oiled waves. "What you need," he continued, looking back at Amy, "is a completely new cut." He combed his long fingers through her hair again. "That *Little House on the Prairie* look is definitely out. Trust me."

Amy, gratified that she'd created any look at all, decided she would trust him. After all, Harvey was the one holding the scissors.

Taking a deep breath, she said, "Do whatever you think best." Alarmed at the way his cold blue eyes suddenly lit up, she added hastily, "But I'm a schoolteacher and I have to set a good example. Don't shave my head or do anything too drastic."

Harvey sniffed. Quickly he combed her hair, dividing and pinning the long lengths into sections. "So, you're a teacher. What grade do you teach?"

Amy blew a piece of hair out of her mouth. "Seventh, eighth and ninth grades. Home economics."

"Indeed!" Harvey paused, silver comb poised above her wet head. "My son is in junior high."

"Oh?" She repeated the monosyllable at spaced intervals for the next thirty minutes as clumps of hair drifted to the floor in silent accompaniment to Harvey's running commentary about Junior. Junior was an A student. He was voted the most popular boy in his class. He was a champion chess player. The anecdotes grew longer, her hair shorter. Harvey realized the importance of family, Amy concluded. She tried to imagine her own father raving about his daughter to a stranger. She couldn't. Her father had always been too involved in his career as a space engineer to spare much thought for anything else. Even his new wife took second place to his work.

A familiar loneliness gripped Amy, and resolutely she pushed the feeling aside. Soon, if all went according to plan, she'd find a husband and he'd put his family before his career, she vowed to herself.

Harvey's voice interrupted her thoughts. "Junior is a whiz at math, and he's led his football team in touchdowns for the last two years."

Her expression must have revealed her surprise at this last revelation because he confided, "He's built like his mother—tall with broad shoulders." The steel comb flicked along Amy's bare nape. "We're a very traditional family. My wife stays home and takes care of the house while I work. But I always make sure I set aside time to spend with my son." His face clouded. "At least, we used to spend time together. Now Junior is too busy. I think he's ashamed of my career." He frowned and twisted the curls on the top of her head into tousled disarray.

"That's pretty common in my experience," Amy said in an effort to alleviate his troubled look. "The kids are testing their wings—establishing their identity. All of them seem to be self-conscious about their parents." She peeked out between the damp strands hanging before her eyes. "We even had a kid whose dad was a major league pitcher. Did the kid brag about it? No way. He didn't want any pressure from his coach to be a star."

She smiled as Harvey's blue eyes met hers in the mirror. He smiled back briefly before his face settled into its austere lines. His expression no longer intimidated Amy, however, and she chatted with him about her decision to revise her appearance—another mistake, she discovered, when her hair was finished. An indifferent Harvey might be brutal; a helpful Harvey was overpowering.

"But I've never had acrylic nails before," she protested weakly as Harvey escorted her to the manicurist.

"It's never too late to improve your appearance," he said. His tone remained firm as he lectured Amy, trapped with her hands in a moisturizing lotion, on proper hair care.

Inspired by his captive audience, he enlarged his theme to include advice on the proper colors to wear. As the manicurist carefully applied the nails, Amy tried to concentrate on what Harvey was saying, wishing she had her hands free to take notes. She wasn't to wear yellow; Harvey gave her yellow T-shirt and jeans a contemptuous look. Stick to the "blue-based" darker colors or pastels and she'd look fine. Accent with silver.

"Wear darker lipstick," he said bluntly. "Play up your eyes more. Go to the mall and talk to a makeup consultant. Believe me, yours is definitely all wrong. For the finishing touch, get your ears pierced. In fact, if you're done, Judy could do it right now."

He snapped his fingers in the air to draw the woman's attention. Amy, drawing on her depleted willpower, clutched his arm to stop him. To try to achieve beauty, she'd already spent six long months starving herself to a smaller size and sixty longer minutes being with Harvey. Earlobe surgery was where she drew the line.

Harvey flinched as her new nails dug into his skin. "Oh, don't bother her! She's busy and I'd rather wait," Amy said.

He raised his pale brows, and she added reluctantly, "I've never been able to stand the idea of a needle being poked in my skin." The thought, to be more specific, made her feel faint.

"Needle!" Harvey scoffed, "We don't use needles anymore."

Her clutch on his arm eased. "You don't?"

"Of course not. We use a gun that shoots the earring through your ear."

"A gun!" Amy released him, both hands flying up to cover her ears protectively. "Oh, no, Never mind. I'll definitely wait."

"It's your decision, of course." He peered down his thin nose at her disapprovingly. To atone, she bought another bottle of conditioner, adding it to the stock he considered essential to maintain "happy" hair.

Escaping finally into the warm afternoon sunshine, Amy climbed into her car and started the engine. She felt naked and vulnerable with her neck and ears exposed. Resolutely, she ignored the feeling. She pulled her purse off her shoulder, nicking her soft cheek with a hard, red nail. She ignored that, too.

Grimly, she focused on one thought as she headed for the stores in Newport Fashion Island. Soon she'd find the man of her dreams. She had a new look, and more important, she had Jake's help and encouragement.

It wouldn't be long now.

* * *

Jake tugged off his muddy work boots, dropping them on the front porch of the bungalow in accordance with one of the new rules Amy had instigated during the past week. He sat for a minute longer on the porch glider, contentedly wiggling his toes in his worn white socks to ease his tired feet. He didn't mind removing his boots on the porch; it made sense not to track mud through the house.

He also didn't mind cutting his day shorter than usual. After she threatened to quit cooking if he was late again, he made sure he was home in time for dinner. Juicy, perfectly prepared meats, vegetables and homemade desserts were a distinct improvement on bouillon soup.

He leaned back, crossed his ankles and gently rocked the glider with his heel. All in all, having Amy here was working out much better than he'd anticipated. She had breakfast ready when he got up, and dinner ready when he got home. She even made him lunches that had his crew begging for a taste.

To be honest, the only problem with the whole setup was a minor one: he hadn't found a date. Which wasn't surprising since he hadn't tried. The more he thought about it—and he thought about it a lot—the more convinced he became that this "manhunt" was just a crazy phase. If he kept putting her off and avoiding her queries as he'd been doing the past week, sooner or later she was bound to forget about it.

He frowned as he felt a prickle of guilt. Okay, maybe it wasn't the most honest thing to do. Still, it was for her own good. Things were fine the way they were. Amy wasn't like other women. She didn't care about fancy clothes or makeup, or the little tricks women used to attract a man. She'd never been "boy crazy" when she was young or even dated much when she was older. This was a phase. Amy was Amy. Casual, easy to be with, exasperating but sometimes a laugh a minute. All he was doing was thinking of her welfare.

His conscience eased, he stood up, stretched and headed into the house. Pushing open the wooden door, he froze in shock.

Amy—a new Amy—was waiting to greet him.

The familiar Amy who had unruly hair and wore casual clothes with cheerful unconcern was nowhere in sight. In her place was a woman who exuded controlled sophistication from the top of her shiny golden-brown curls to the soles of her three-inch black heels. Her tight-fitting red dress appeared simple with a scooped neckline and elbow-length sleeves, but there was nothing simple about the way it accentuated her petite figure.

Jake's wide eyes quickly scanned high small breasts, a slim waist and curvy hips. He dragged his gaze away, only to have it caught by long, shapely legs encased in silky black hose. His firm mouth tightened as she pivoted and he glimpsed the seam line running up the back of her calf.

He jerked his gaze to her face. That too was different. Her bright blue gaze returned his, searching for a reaction. She'd covered up the freckles scattered on her small nose. She'd even done something to her eyes—he wasn't sure what, but her dark brown lashes were now black and there was shimmery blue stuff on her eyelids.

He looked down at her lips, outlined in the same shade as her dress. Unwillingly captivated, he watched her red mouth purse, then part slightly, revealing small white teeth. He was jolted from his perusal as she demanded suddenly, "Well, what do you think?"

He thought she looked older. He thought she looked polished. Hell, he even thought she looked sophisticated. She just didn't look like Amy.

And he missed the old Amy.

"Think about what?" He stepped around her to hang up his jacket on the hook by the door.

Amy rolled her eyes. "About the way I look, of course. Don't tell me you haven't noticed the difference." She twirled and Jake guiltily lifted his eyes from her curved bottom.

She faced him again and he frowned. Stepping forward he caught her chin and tilted it up to assess the small red mark on her cheek. "How did that happen?

"Oh, I nicked myself with my new nails." Amy pulled away from him, lifting her hands for inspection.

He gave a low whistle. "My God, those are killers! Why on earth did you have those put on?"

"Well, Harvey—"

"Who the hell is Harvey?"

"Harvey's my hairdresser," she said, and Jake's tense stance relaxed. She continued, "He gave me some very good advice about fashion."

"He didn't give you good advice if he convinced you to wear those nails."

"You have something against long nails?"

"They're stupid. And if the scratch on your cheek is any indication, they're dangerous, too."

"How strange." Amy crossed her arms and intently examined the nails in question. "You didn't seem to be worried about danger when that woman you brought to Maddie's that time—Judy, wasn't it?—ran nails like these through your hair.''

An angry red flush crept under Jake's brown cheeks. "Fine. You want to have long nails—have long nails.''

Slightly ashamed of her remark, she said, "I don't want to argue with you. Let's just agree to disagree about my nails." He strode past her toward the kitchen, and she muttered under her breath, "Until you realize you're wrong." Jake stopped and gave her a hard look. Amy, innocently buffing her nails against the shoulder of her dress, pretended not to notice.

Jake shoved open the bedroom door, and Amy's heels tapped quickly on the hardwood floor behind him.

"Okay, so what about my hair? How do you think it looks?" She followed him into the bedroom, watching as he opened the closet.

Yanking a clean shirt from a hanger, he turned and studied her hair. Silently, he decided he did like it. It looked cute. Soft. Touchable. It looked . . .

"Short," he said. He turned away and grabbed a pair of jeans.

"Short!" Bewildered by his flat tones, Amy plopped into a chair. "Jake, I know it's short. Is that all you can say?"

"It looks nice. Fine. Great."

"You don't sound like you think it looks great."

Jake slammed the closet door, cursing as it bounced back open. His dark brows lowered over his eyes. "I said it looked great—what do you want from me? Do you think I should make up a song and dance about it or something?"

Amy didn't answer.

Unreasonably angry at her silence, he bit out, "Tell me what you want to hear. You look wonderful—fabulous! Ready to go out and find a man—a hundred men!"

More silence.

Angrily, he watched as she looked down at a loose thread in her dress, plucking aimlessly at it with a long, red nail. He opened his mouth to goad her again when she glanced at him.

His mouth snapped shut.

The blue eyes, minutes before so happily expectant, were full of hurt. Her red mouth quivered. Jake's throat constricted as he wearily dragged his fingers through his hair. "I'm sorry, Amy."

Her mouth trembled harder and tears filled her eyes. Jake groaned, pulling her into his arms. Her body felt small and soft against him. At least she still felt like the Amy he knew.

Amy pressed her face in his shirt. Inhaling the warm smell of sawdust and man, she enjoyed the comfort of Jake's strong arms. His deep voice rumbled from beneath her cheek. "Aw, hell, Amy. Don't cry. I didn't mean to jump all over you like that. It's just been a bad day."

Unappeased, she buried her face deeper into his hard chest and sniffed.

Jake rested his rough chin on her sweet-smelling curls and tried harder. "Okay, if you want the truth, you look beautiful. I guess I just kind of liked the old Amy. I'm not sure all these changes you've made are for the better."

Amy lifted her head to stare at him, her lashes forming wet spikes around her surprised eyes. "What can be so wrong about changing my clothes and hair-style?''

Jake shrugged, unable to put his uneasiness into words. It seemed he didn't know Amy like he'd always thought he did. He'd only recently come to terms with the inward changes in her and now she was hitting him with outward changes, too. He rocked her gently back and forth, searching for the words to explain his feeling of loss. He couldn't find them. ''Nothing, I suppose,'' he admitted finally. ''As long as you're making changes that you want to make and not because this guy…Harvey—'' he bit the name out with disgust ''—talks you into them.''

Amy peeked up at him. ''Well, I didn't let him talk me into piercing my ears. But maybe the nails weren't a good idea.''

''Yeah.''

''The haircut looks good, doesn't it?''

''Yeah.''

She studied his set face a little uncertainly. ''Do you still want to help me meet some eligible men? If it's too much trouble, the book suggests a few places I could—''

''No.'' His arms tightened suddenly, then loosened. He gave her a final squeeze and stepped back. ''I said I'd introduce you to a couple of guys, and I will. Just give me a few days.''

Chapter Four

Fourteen days. Could it really be that long since he'd promised Amy he'd find her a date? Jake leaned back in his office swivel chair, linking his hands behind his head. Frowning, he stared at the man seated across the steel desk.

Shorty shifted uneasily under his boss's penetrating regard. Running a broad hand over his sunburned forehead, he touched his battered baseball cap and quickly yanked it off, his round face reddening beneath his freckles.

Still frowning, Jake leaned forward to study a paper on the desk while Shorty twisted his cap into a crumpled ball, smoothing it back out against the thigh of his beige carpenter overalls. He set the cap down and began cracking his knuckles, stopping abruptly as Jake stood up.

"So, Shorty, you've been with me for five years now."

"Yep." Shorty leaned forward. He picked up the cap again and turned it slowly, resting his elbows on his knees.

"We went through some hard times at first."

"Yep."

"You're a good worker. I've been lucky to have you."

Another red tide flooded Shorty's face. "Thanks."

Leaning back again, Jake concentrated on aligning a supply bill with the edge of the desk. "You know, sometimes I get so busy, it's hard for me to keep up with how things are going." He glanced up. "How are things going with you?"

"Fine." Obviously relieved to have the conversation proceed along familiar lines, Shorty relaxed a little. "We've got a good start on the Alton place."

"Yeah, great." Jake carefully lined up a blue pencil with the paper. "But how are things going with you personally?"

Shorty stiffened. The cap turned faster. "Personally?"

"Yeah. Are you still dating . . . uh, Cindy—"

"Sue." The cap stopped.

"That's right. Sue."

"No."

"Oh." Jake abandoned the pencil and leaned forward across the desk. "Are you involved with anyone else?"

"No." A puzzled crease formed between Shorty's brows.

"Great!" Jake said heartily. "That's just great! Well, keep up the good work and I'll see you out at the job later today or on Monday."

Uncertainly, Shorty stood up. Pulling on his cap, he walked to the door, but halfway there he stopped and turned back to Jake. "Boss, can I ask you something?"

"Sure. Go ahead." Jake straightened.

"Are you gonna be talking with all the guys? I know you brought in Waring and Mendez, and to tell the truth, Jake, they didn't know what the hell is going on anymore than I do. Is there a problem or something, because if there is," he said, shifting uneasily, "maybe you should let us in on it."

"Honestly, there's no problem." Jake rose and strode across the room. Slapping the other man reassuringly on the shoulder, he repeated, "No problem at all."

Shorty left, a look of relief on his face. Jake remained in the middle of the room, cursing softly and staring at the closed door. He stopped abruptly as the door swung wide and Rosie, his secretary, marched in.

"I heard that, Jake," she said sternly, as he retreated behind his desk to the safety of his chair.

Jake tried an intimidating look, but Rosie, whose steel backbone extended from the top of her iron-gray head to the soles of her size-nine feet, frowned right back at him. Jake groaned. Rosie had been with his company from the beginning, and she was no more impressed with the million-dollar business he now owned—or with him—than she'd been with the naive young man she'd worked with in a rented cubicle.

Her round face wrinkled pugnaciously. "Now, why are you interrogating the single men?" she demanded.

"I'm not interrogating them."

"Call it what you want—the men are worried." Rosie folded her plump arms across an equally plump bosom. "They think you are either going to lay someone off or—and this is the popular view—that you're losing your mind. After Rod told me yesterday some of the questions you've been asking, I agree with the majority. What do you care if he likes kids or not? Or if he's seeing anyone? What are you up to, Jake Joseph Weston?" She shoved her pink glasses up on her high-bridged nose and stared at him accusingly.

When Rosie, a crony of his grandmother, used his middle name, she meant business. Jake raked an impatient hand through his hair and admitted, "I'm just checking to see if any of them are interested in going on a date."

"What!"

"With a friend of mine, for goodness' sake! A girl friend!"

"What friend?" Rosie narrowed her eyes and gave a disapproving sniff.

"Amy Larkin—the girl who lived next door to Maddie. You know her, you've talked to her on the phone. She wants to meet an 'eligible' man and I've agreed to try and help her."

Rosie looked at him thoughtfully. "Why don't you take her out yourself?" she asked.

Jake snorted. "Amy is an old friend. The closest thing I have to a sister. She's a good buddy, but we'd mix sexually like oil and water. Anyway, I'm not interested in marriage. I don't have the time to devote to a wife or, heaven forbid, a family."

"Why did you rule out Waring, Mendez and Shorty?"

Jake shifted under Rosie's sharp eyes. "Mendez is involved with someone and Waring isn't reliable. He runs through beach bunnies at the rate of two a week."

"And Shorty?"

"Shorty wasn't right, either."

"Why not?"

"He's just not." Jake picked up a pen, studying the supply billing in a broad hint that the conversation was over.

Rosie didn't take the hint. "What's wrong with Shorty?"

Exasperated, Jake threw the pen down. "Nothing's wrong with Shorty. He just isn't right."

"I see. Well, luckily, I know someone who is," Rosie said briskly. "Richard John Lowell."

"Richard Lowell?" Jake frowned. "Do I know him?"

"He's my nephew—an accountant. He's a little shy and he doesn't date much. It would be nice for him to meet a sweet young lady like Amy. I'll call him right now, you just check with Amy and decide on a night." She paused, reading the doubt on Jake's face. "Don't worry, Jake. He's a nice boy. Nothing will go wrong."

"Yeah, I know." What could he say? The guy, who sounded like a jerk to him, was Rosie's nephew. It wasn't a good solution—still it was better than nothing.

Feeling strangely restless, Jake gathered the papers scattered on his desk into a pile and stood up. "I think I'll head on home."

Rosie's gray brows shot up toward her crimped bangs. "Head home? Jake, it's only eight-thirty. You just got here less than an hour ago."

"It's Saturday and the guys will be breaking early," he pointed out. "I think I'll go home and pick up the truck later. It's only six miles, and I haven't run this past week." Rosie continued to stare at him. He put his hands on his hips. "What's wrong with that?"

Rosie's brows rose even higher at his sharp tone. "Did I say anything was wrong?" Her eyes narrowed speculatively behind her thick lenses.

Feeling hunted, Jake brushed past her. In the shower room adjacent to the office he changed into navy-blue trunks and escaped into the morning fog.

He jogged through the block-long business section of prime real estate crowding the ocean, his shoes pounding rhythmically on the concrete. As he reached the beach, he turned to run on the hard-packed sand along the shoreline.

The fog would burn off by noon under the hot summer sun, he decided. Now it shrouded the beach in a gray blanket, muting the crash of waves and the shrill cries of the gulls circling overhead.

Jake shivered as the mist sent a chill running down his bare chest. Not even halfway through the six-mile run and already his thigh muscles ached. He grimaced. Talk about being out of shape. Running daily was a part of his routine—or what used to be his routine. Since Amy's arrival, several of his usual activities had been neglected.

Reaching the pier, he ran up the bank along massive weather-beaten posts and turned smoothly onto the planks leading out over the water. His shoes slapped briskly along the rough wood, sending gulls and pigeons shrieking into the air. Automatically, he lengthened his stride to avoid the rancid bait discarded by the fishermen bending over the wooden rails on either side. Circling the faded gray restaurant at the end of the pier, he headed back.

He couldn't really blame Amy for upsetting his schedule. After all, it wasn't her fault that he'd begun leaving work a little early each day. It was just kind of... comforting, for want of a better word, to have someone waiting when he came home.

Yeah, that was it. Home. Somehow, Amy had transformed the beach house into a home. He wasn't sure how she'd done it, but not since his mother was alive had he returned to a house that was so welcoming: a house filled with the tart lemony smell of furniture polish and the warm, sweet aromas of baking. And, best of all, a smiling woman to joke with or complain about his day to. Visits to Maddie had kept the memory of his parents alive, but living with Amy renewed nostalgic emotions he'd thought long buried under the daily grind of business.

Living with Amy was easy, he decided. When she wasn't cleaning or cooking she seemed perfectly content to spend her days shopping for clothes, sunbathing and, of course, studying her damn book.

And that was the problem. That damn book. Amy was biding her time, but she hadn't yet abandoned her stupid husband hunt as he'd hoped she would. For the past week she'd given him skeptical looks every time he'd assured her that, yes, he *did* have someone in mind, and, no he was *not* stalling. And he wasn't. Not really. It was just that he'd never noticed before that the guys he knew had so many faults. Definitely too many faults to go out with Amy.

So far, he'd managed to keep the truth from her and ignore the accusing glances she gave him across the dinner table. Glances that were almost enough to make the delicious meals she created turn to ashes in his mouth. But not quite.

Thinking of the meals Amy prepared, his stomach—an inch wider than two weeks ago—began to growl. Sternly, Jake tightened his abdominal muscles and increased his pace, his lungs burning from the cold, salty air. A foamy wave rolled up, almost touching his feet, and receded. He moved up the bank onto drier sand.

On the shore again, he slowed, each step in the sand increasing the pull on his calf muscles. Amy'd probably be ecstatic to learn he'd found her a date—or, rather, that Rosie had. Maybe he'd tell her when he got home. Then again, maybe he'd wait. No, he would tell her.

When the time was right.

Leaving the shoreline, Jake ran across the beach and jumped the low wall that separated sand from sidewalk. In the gray morning, a light shone ahead through the window of his bungalow and his pace increased.

At the beach house, he stopped, bent at the waist and breathed deeply before quickly rinsing off under the outside shower. His chest muscles twitched at the stinging of the cold water, while the muscles in his thighs tightened at the sudden cessation of movement. Grabbing a towel out of a shallow cupboard holding beach chairs, he wiped off and then walked around the path and opened the front door.

Immediately the smell of freshly baked doughnuts assaulted his senses. Sniffing appreciatively, he headed toward the kitchen.

"Amy?"

"In here," she answered. Dressed in her faded pink robe, she sat at the kitchen table with a book—the book, Jake noted in passing disgust—resting against the plate of powdered doughnuts in front of her. "Back already?"

"Yeah. I cut it short today." He headed for the refrigerator and Amy returned to her reading. Still breathing deeply, Jake removed a carton of milk. Leaning back against the counter, he turned to Amy as he popped it open and took a drink.

She looked—he straightened, his eyes widening in surprise—hell, she looked great.

Sunbathing had lightened her tumbled curls, and the bright chestnut strands gleamed from the overhead kitchen light. Her face, bare of makeup, was tinted the delicate shade of golden oak.

Jake's muscles tightened as she glanced at him and smiled. Against her darkened skin, her eyes seemed bluer, her teeth whiter. A few more freckles were scattered across her smooth cheeks and nose. And her lips—Jake took another large swallow in an effort to relieve the constriction in his throat—her lips were the color of red-stained cedar.

His lower body surged powerfully when her pink tongue suddenly darted out to lick the sugar powdering her top lip. He took a large mouthful of milk, holding the cold liquid in his mouth. In a vain effort to cool the blood throbbing through his body, he lifted the icy milk carton to the side of his hot face. *This is my grandmother's friend,* he reminded himself forcefully, *who can make my life hell at times. Not the most sexually arousing woman I've ever seen.*

Unaware of his reaction, Amy returned to her book. A look of concentration filled her face, and she said absently, "Jake, listen to this. It's really interesting."

Keeping her place in the book with a slim finger, she read, "Scientists have found that a man whose heart is beating faster than normal from some form of physical exercise is more attracted to a good-looking woman."

Jake choked, and milk spewed across the kitchen. Startled, Amy jumped out of her chair and ran to where he stood, coughing and sputtering, bracing himself against the counter.

"Oh, my goodness. What happened? Don't worry! I know the Heimlich maneuver." Undeterred by his efforts to ward her off, Amy planted herself behind him, bracing her bare feet and linking her slim arms in front of his broad, bare torso.

Jake shuddered as he felt her warm breasts pushing against his cold back. The tiny nubs of her nipples poked at him through her thin robe, while his buttocks bumped against her stomach and pelvis. Still coughing, he redoubled his attempts to free himself without hurting her.

Alarmed by his erratic movements, Amy tightened her grip. For a few seconds they swayed and struggled, until Jake grasped her wrists, loosening her hold. Breaking away, he grabbed a kitchen towel and wiped his streaming mouth.

"Dammit, Amy! You're going to kill me one of these days!" he said hoarsely. "Don't ever do that again." He sat down in her abandoned chair.

"I was just trying to help!"

"Well, don't."

"Fine. I won't."

He wearily rubbed his face. Amy watched him a moment with her hands on her hips before offering, "I'll get you a dry towel and a shirt."

She hurried out of the room, leaving Jake alone with the book. He eyed it warily, then reluctantly picked it up, turning it over to the place Amy had quoted.

A minute later, he slammed it shut. Absently, he rubbed his jaw as he reviewed the facts. He'd been jogging. His heart had been beating faster. And finally—irrefutably—he'd seen Amy, and the sexual response he'd felt had sizzled through him like a jolt of electricity.

Just like in the study.

Apparently, the book was no hoax. As the only fish in a very small pond, Jake reassured himself, it was natural he'd be nibbling the bait Amy—albeit unknowingly—was dangling. But unless he wanted to end up "hooked," he'd better quit circling and introduce more males into his "little pal's" sphere of influence. Fast.

Amy returned, handing him a clean towel and a blue shirt. As he wiped his face, he studied her expression from beneath lowered lids, but could only discern traces of rapidly fading concern.

"Are you okay now?" She perched on the edge of the table, casually swinging her slender, brown legs.

"Yeah." As okay as you could get with a raging libido. He pulled the shirt over his head and then chanced another look. Dammit, she still looked great. He averted his eyes from her cute toes and determinedly picked up a doughnut. "So, what were you telling me about?"

"Oh, the book." Amy picked it up and the pretty blonde on the cover beamed at Jake. He glared back. "Well, the study says if you want your date to find you more attractive, you should try to get his heart rate up. Do something active with him like going skating, jogging, skiing, biking, tennis—whatever."

Reading on, she frowned. "But it also says the effect can be negative as well, and a man will be more repulsed by a woman who is below average in appearance." She looked at him, her blue eyes anxious. "I don't think I'm below-average, do you?"

"No."

"Thanks. But Jake, are you sure? I mean, after all, you've known me for so long that if I am below-average, maybe you've just gotten used to it."

Jake found he was sitting eye level with her chest and, more important, her peaked nipples. "Trust me on this. You're not."

Amy smiled at him. "Well, thanks again."

"No problem." He shoved the rest of the doughnut into his mouth. It was time to stock the fish pond and get off the hook. "I've got great news. I've found you a date."

Amy's eyes widened. "You did! Who is it?" She hopped off the table and stood tensely before him. "*When* is it?"

Jake decided silently that the sooner Richard John Lowell arrived, the sooner he himself could overcome this strange attraction he was feeling. "He's probably coming tonight. I have to make a phone call."

Giving the book a final baleful look, he strode out of the room.

Chapter Five

"Amy!"

"Coming!" Spurred into action by Jake's voice, Amy ignored the pile of clothes she'd been agonizing over for the past hour and snatched up a pair of jeans. Jake said he'd told Richard to wear casual and comfortable clothes. What could be more comfortable than jeans?

Forget comfortable; the jeans were tight. Flinging herself back on the four-poster bed, she tugged the zipper up as gravity flattened her tummy. Standing again, she did a couple of deep knee bends, breathing a little easier as the newly washed denim stretched.

Jake's voice rumbled up the stairs, and she quickly pulled a white short-sleeved sweater over her head and brushed her flattened curls into tousled disarray. She sprayed cologne indiscriminately on her throat and wrists as the door to the stairway opened.

"Amy!"

"I'm coming!"

Shoes. Shoes were a necessity. Amy groped under the bed for her sandals and her sweater became streaked with dust. Swearing under her breath, she yanked the sweater over her head and grabbed a pink blouse. Frantically, she fluffed her hair again as the door opened below.

"Amy!"

Amy yelled back, "I said I'm coming!" She took a calming breath and studied her reflection in the wavy mirror above the dresser. The pants fit snugly. The pink blouse accentuated her newly acquired tan. Her hair was shining and her makeup applied just as the salesclerk had advised.

She assumed what the book called optimum posture for attracting men: shoulders back, chest out, legs straight, tummy in, back arched; and bottom pushed out just a tad. She held the pose and looked at her reflection again. This was as good as it got; better, in fact, than it had ever been.

Too bad the idea of going on a date with a complete stranger held as much appeal as washing dirty socks.

Her shoulders slumped. She might as well face it, she wasn't excited about this date. She knew what the problem was, had known in fact, since she'd tangled with it in the kitchen this morning. The problem devoured eight doughnuts at a sitting, had a teasing grin, understanding gray eyes and went by the name of Jake.

Amy sighed. Through the years she must have hugged Jake a hundred times. Not once had she felt the way she had earlier this morning when she thought he was choking. Panic at his distress had mingled with a warm desire ignited by the feel of his smooth, hard back pressing against her breasts and tummy.

It was the desire that scared her.

How many times had she heard her mother say, "Don't make the same mistake I made, Amelia. Use your head when you select a husband. Don't be carried away thinking you're in love, because when infatuation burns out, you may have to live with your mistake for a long time." Invariably, the words were directed over Amy's head at her father. Amy, remembering her father's indifferent stare at her mother's bitter words, shivered. They'd been unhappy; she'd never doubted that—nor the fact that she was the only reason they stayed together.

They'd loved her, she supposed, in their own fashion. But home had always been filled with unhappiness; a place to escape from. Loneliness, Amy had discovered at an early age, could exist even in a house filled with people.

Coming here had definitely been a mistake. She would not end up like her mother with a man she was incompatible with, a man who resented being married and cared more for his business than his family. What she felt for Jake was merely an illusion, a prime example of what the book called, "letting lust lead you to the wrong man."

Jake, no doubt about it, was the wrong man. Oh, she'd admit he had a sense of humor, albeit misguided. But not one other of her requirements did he fill. She grimly ticked them off on her fingers. He was over the age limit. He was domineering and often chauvinistic. He'd never given the least inclination of liking children or wanting a family. He was a workaholic. To top it all off, he viewed her as a generic kid sister and a troublesome one at that.

Perhaps she'd subconsciously hoped he'd fall for her new image. At the very least, he might have hesitated about setting her up with another man. Instead, he'd almost leapt for the phone after waving her out of the room that morning. He'd frowned when she'd asked him to let Richard know that she'd gotten tickets for Disneyland, but that was probably because Jake had old-fashioned ideas about a man paying for his date. Jake would never let a woman pay.

Stop it! she told her reflection sternly. *No more comparisons of Jake and other men.* In a case like this, the book advised using positive "self-talk."

Squaring her shoulders again, Amy thought, *You are happy and excited.* All this was *your* idea. This is going to be *fun.* You are not nervous. No one is nervous on a first date anymore.

Silently she repeated her pep talk as she walked down the stairs and through the kitchen and dining room. Entering the living room, she considered saying it once more, aloud this time, for the benefit of her date.

"Amy, this is Rosie's nephew, Richard Lowell. Richard, Amy." Jake's tones were clipped as he performed the introductions.

Richard John Lowell rose politely when she came in. Amy glanced up to greet her date, and then looked up even higher. Richard had to be at least six feet, seven inches tall. Catching sight of Amy's petite figure, he looked as miserable as a giraffe being hunted by a pygmy.

Tall and thin, he appeared even more so next to Jake's broad and tightly muscled frame. Not only did

Richard look miserable, dressed in a formal navy-blue suit, white shirt and pin-striped tie, he also looked hot. At least, Amy hoped it was the summer night and not nervousness that had caused perspiration to bead on his high pale forehead.

He hunched his head and shoulders forward in an almost apologetic manner as he gently shook hands with her. Looking up into his anxious, soft brown eyes, Amy's own nervousness melted away. She wasn't the only one who hated blind dates. Richard exhibited all the uneasiness of a teenager on his first day in her class. She immediately began chatting to put him at ease.

Jake shifted restlessly in his chair as Amy chuckled at something Richard said. When he'd met the other man at the door, he'd thought the guy was nice. He'd felt that way until Amy came tripping down the stairs dressed in tight jeans that molded the slim curve of her bottom. The more the two laughed together, the more Jake decided he'd been wrong, very wrong, about Richard. Judging by the way his eyes lit up in response to Amy's smiles, the man was a wolf in sheep's clothing. If Amy couldn't realize it, then it was up to Jake to rectify the situation.

He interrupted Richard's humorous recital of the stress accountants suffer from at tax time to ask, "Would you like a beer, Richard?"

Surprised by his abrupt tone, Amy shot him a questioning glance. Never before had she heard him sound so unfriendly to a stranger. For goodness' sake, this was Rosie's nephew!

Jake avoided her eyes, fastening his gaze on the other man, who responded politely, "No, thank you. I'm afraid beer doesn't agree with me."

"Soft drink? Orange juice?" Jake persisted.

"I'm afraid I have a rather delicate digestive system."

Jake opened his mouth to make another remark, and Amy quickly cut him off. "So, Richard, I guess we got our dress codes mixed." She smiled. "I have tickets to Disneyland, but maybe you had somewhere else in mind?"

"Actually, no. The park is fine." Richard smiled at Amy. The smile faded as he turned to Jake. "I guess I misunderstood you. I thought you said Amy preferred to dress formally when she went to the amusement park."

It seemed to Amy a fleeting look of guilt crossed Jake's face. His voice, however, showed no trace of it as he replied. "I did? Are you sure?"

Richard wasn't. "Maybe I misunderstood." He turned back to Amy. "I wish I had worn something a little more casual. I'm afraid a suit isn't appropriate. I'd just leave my jacket behind, but it tends to cool as the sun sets and I am prone to chills."

"Chills, too? What a shame," Jake said, before Amy could answer. "Maybe you two should forget the Disneyland idea. Might catch a cold, ruin your suit. Why don't you two spend the evening here? I think there's a Dodger game on the tube. You a Dodger fan, Richard?"

"Well, actually—"

"Actually," Amy broke in smoothly, "I'm looking forward to getting out." Amy's smile at Richard warmed up several degrees. "If you're worried about damaging your suit or catching cold, I think I have a solution." She directed an icy stare at Jake. "Jake, can he borrow your jacket?"

"Huh?" Caught off guard by Amy's sudden attack, Jake looked wary. "What jacket?"

"You know. Your old leather jacket."

"My *leather* jacket?"

"Yes."

"The jacket I've had since college?"

"Yes."

"The jacket I wear to work every day?"

"Yes."

Richard said hurriedly, "I wouldn't want to impose..."

"Nonsense, it's no imposition." Amy patted his hand. "It's only a jacket. You don't have a problem sharing your jacket, do you, Jake?" she persisted.

He answered through gritted teeth, "No, no problem at all."

Ignoring his glare, Amy walked over to the hook by the door. She brought the faded brown jacket to Richard, who pulled off his suit coat. He tugged at his tie, then gestured helplessly at it as he bent toward her. "I tied it rather tight. I don't suppose that you'd mind..."

"Of course not," Amy answered. Jake frowned as she stood on her tiptoes and deftly unknotted the tie. The frown became a scowl as she helped Richard pull on his old leather jacket.

Stepping back, Amy observed the fit of the jacket on Richard's thinner frame. Since Jake's shoulders were the broader of the two, the jacket sleeves covered Richard's long arms. Pleased with how the garment gave him an almost rakish look, she said, "It looks good!" She grinned at Richard who smiled back. Jake took another long drink of beer.

"Well, we'd better be on our way," Amy said. Turning, she gathered up her beaded denim jacket and matching purse, and headed toward the door with Richard. "Bye, Jake," she called over her shoulder and walked out.

"Bye, Amy. Ah, Richard..." Jake paused and the other man looked back inquiringly.

Jake's voice deepened. "The jacket isn't really important. Amy is. Take care of her and don't stay out too late."

"Don't worry, I will. I mean, I won't. I mean, don't worry, I'll take good care of your sister."

"She's not my sister."

"Cousin?"

"Nope." Jake stretched, causing his black T-shirt to strain across his broad chest. "Amy and I are what you'd call...good friends."

Richard's long face settled back into melancholy lines. "I see." Perspiration beading his forehead again, he hurried after Amy.

Sitting on the couch four hours later, Jake reached forward and picked up a beer off the coffee table. Leaning back, he gazed at the silently flickering television as he took a swallow. The Dodger game was tied and running into the twelfth inning. Usually he'd be on the edge of his seat; tonight he just didn't give a damn.

It would be nice if he were drunk, he decided. Then he'd be able to forget how he'd acted like a teenage macho jerk earlier when Amy and Richard left on their date. The warm beer in his hand, however, was the same one he'd been drinking when Amy came downstairs looking eager and sexy. The jealousy that had surged up unexpectedly was still simmering, but had cooled enough to make him feel like a fool for his earlier behavior.

Never before had he been possessive about any woman. The feeling had taken him by surprise, causing him to act in an unfamiliar way.

He considered blaming his rude behavior on Richard but reluctantly abandoned the idea. Not only was Richard Rosie's nephew, he seemed like a harmless guy—the kind anyone would be glad to have take out his sister. It was just Jake's own bad luck that Amy wasn't really his sister.

He took a drink, grimacing at the flat taste. No, it was time to face up to the facts, put the blame where it belonged. He'd acted like a jerk, and there was only one person responsible.

Amy.

Pleased with his deduction, Jake balanced the warm can on his abdomen as he reviewed the ways Amy was disrupting his life. He'd gained weight. His employees thought he was crazy. She'd dragged him into her idiotic hunt for a husband. Worst of all, she'd been here less than a month, and he found himself concentrating more on her than his work. Never before had a woman distracted him from his job.

Now she'd gone on one date with a nice guy, and he was ready to jump in his truck to go search for her. And he would, if she didn't get home before midnight, which meant...Jake squinted at his watch in the darkened room...she had fifteen minutes. How long did amusement parks stay open these days, anyway?

He was searching for the phone book to call and find out when car headlights flashed in the front window. Jake froze, then hastily shoved papers back into the small telephone table by the door. Car doors slammed outside. Footsteps and voices traveled up the front walk. Crouching, he tried to determine his best course of action. Should he go to bed? Naw. The guy might decide to stay awhile then. Should he open the door? Pretend to watch the game?

Suddenly, he became aware the footsteps had stopped and the voices were quiet. Too quiet. He strained, but could only hear a rustling sound, like a paper bag being dropped on the porch. What the hell was going on? Amy couldn't be kissing the guy, could she? The thought caused his stomach to ache with sharp intensity.

Still kneeling, he started to lift the curtain on the windowed door. His hand dropped. It would be rude and childish to move the curtain and peek out. No way would he sink that low. But suppose he didn't touch the curtain? Surely, no one—specifically, no one by the name of Amy—could blame him for what he saw looking casually out the window. Angling his face to the side, he tried to peer beneath the curtain without touching it. It didn't work; he couldn't see a thing. Turning his head to the other side, he moved closer, his hands still conscientiously at his sides. The doorknob turned, and before he could protect himself, Amy thrust the door open, smacking him in the face.

"Yow!" Jake rolled to his side, both hands covering his face. "Damn it. I dink you bwoke my nose!"

"What!" Amy flipped on the switch. Stunned, she stood in the doorway, looking down at Jake who was sitting on the floor. "Jake, what on earth are you doing?" Her blue eyes narrowed suspiciously. "You weren't spying on me, were you?"

"Of course I wasn't spying on you." Gingerly holding his nose, Jake stood up. "I was looking for the phone book." It sounded reasonable, he realized, pleased. It was even the truth. Sort of.

"Who were you planning on calling?"

"I really don't think that's any of your business," he answered, feeling trapped.

Amy eyed him. "You're right. Good night, Jake." She turned to head upstairs.

"Amy, wait!"

"Yes?" She stopped and looked at him.

"Uh, how was your date?" he asked.

Her eyes glinted. "Please allow me to quote, 'I don't think that's any of your business.' End quote."

She'd started to move away, when he asked, "Where's my jacket?"

She paused. "Oh, yes. Your jacket. I have a confession to make about your old, worn-out jacket."

Foreboding had always been just a word; now Jake knew what it felt like. "What about my jacket?"

"I'm afraid Richard's stomach couldn't tolerate the teacup ride. I'm sorry, but your jacket ended up, shall we say, a little worse for wear?"

Jake deduced flatly, "The guy puked on my jacket."

Amy pursed her lips. "Puke is such a disgusting word." He took a threatening step toward her, and she retreated with her hands held out defensively, her eyes alight with laughter. "I'll get it cleaned, Jake! I promise it will be as good as new. To tell you the truth, I feel partly responsible."

"Why? Did you insist he go on the ride?"

Frowning a little, she shook her head. Her curls bounced. "No, but he looked a little sick when he came out to the car. I should have said something."

"Oh." Jake shifted guiltily.

"Jake..."

"Yeah?" he answered, his voice low, his eyes wary.

"The evening was rather nice, in spite of Richard's problem. Anyway, it wasn't too bad for a start. Thanks for setting it up."

She turned, and Jake's gaze fastened on her pert bottom as she left the room. He sighed.

His nose hurt. His conscience hurt. His jacket was a mess. How many more of Amy's "nice" evenings would he be able to take?

Chapter Six

Jake was late coming home from work the next day.

She certainly didn't care, Amy told herself as she wrapped his cold steak in foil and threw it in the refrigerator. He had his own life to lead. Simply because he'd been home for dinner for the last couple of weeks, didn't mean he'd completely abandoned his workaholic ways.

She paused, holding the refrigerator door open. Maybe he wasn't working. Maybe he had a date. He'd intimated he was calling someone last night. She retrieved the steak and the rest of his meal that she'd just put away and slammed the door shut. Well, that was fine, too. She tossed the steak in the garbage, then scraped mashed potatoes, asparagus and deep-dish apple pie—Jake's favorite—on top of it. What Jake Joseph Weston did with his life was no concern of hers.

Frowning, she picked up her book and popcorn and headed for the living room, where she plopped down in her favorite corner of Jake's massive black couch. The corner was conveniently situated so she could look out the front bay window.

The window framed a view of Jake's sandy front yard, his white picket fence and the narrow street beyond. She wasn't watching for him, Amy assured herself. She just enjoyed counting the number of cars coming down the street. Cars belonging to considerate people who came home at a decent hour.

Fifteen minutes later, Jake's battered pickup rumbled up and parked in front of the house. Amy abandoned her tally to track his progress up the walk. He looked tired. The lines fanning out from his eyes were deepened; his jeans and white T-shirt were covered with dust. He stretched on the front porch, wearily rotating his muscled arms before he bent to pull off his boots. Amy opened her book, her unsettled feeling disappearing now that Jake was home.

She glanced up, smiling when he came in. Jake paused in the doorway. His narrowed gaze pinned her as he asked, "Are you going out tonight?"

She stared at him, and then down at herself. Clearly his question was a rhetorical one. Sprawled on the couch, she had a bowl of popcorn balanced on her stomach and a book propped on her chest. Her faded yellow sweatshirt hung two sizes too big, covering her cutoff shorts that were a deep breath away from a size too small. On her feet were her favorite slippers. Deliberately, she crossed her ankles. "Richard asked me, but I found out he's prone to bunny allergies," she answered solemnly, wiggling her bunny slippers to make their raggedy ears bounce. "Why?"

"Just wondering." Jake looked at her feet, clad in the ridiculous slippers. Despite himself, his mouth twitched.

Amy caught his reaction, and bent her leg to pat one of the slippers on the head. "This one hurt his widdle nose, just like Jake," she said in baby talk. "And how is Jake's widdle nose today?" she inquired, widening her eyes at him.

"Jake's nose is just fine, thank you," he drawled, leaning against the doorjamb and crossing his arms. "And if you say one more word in that nauseating tone, I'll stuff those rabbits down your throat. Or maybe mine, I'm so hungry. Is there anything left from dinner?"

"Sorry, no." Remembering the food she'd dumped in the garbage, Amy guiltily withdrew into her book.

Jake watched her for a moment. His nose hadn't bothered him during the day, but his reaction at the thought of Amy going out on another date with Richard—or any guy, for that matter—had. He'd chafed at the hundred and one delays that had kept him at the job site two hours past quitting time. Working alongside his crew, he'd concocted arguments to logically and calmly convince her to abandon her ridiculous quest for a man.

Now he found the last thing he wanted to do was disturb the oasis of peace Amy had created in the beach house. A light breeze fluffed the starched white curtains at the windows, and the soft light from the setting sun bounced from the polished mahogany end tables to the gleaming oak floor. Amy'd even cleared off the old oak coffee table that doubled as a footstool. The thought of easing his tired body on the couch next to her was so appealing that he decided to forget her whole damn scheme for a while. First he'd shower, grab a sandwich and then enjoy the warm summer evening.

He straightened. "Save me some popcorn," he ordered before he disappeared down the hall.

Ten minutes later he was back, refreshed after his shower and wearing gray sweatpants and a black tank top. Without bothering to look up from her book, Amy obligingly moved her feet to the coffee table when he claimed the other end of the couch.

She was reading her self-help book again, he noted, a little of his sense of well-being fading. He picked up the TV remote control and switched on the baseball game. He propped his bare feet next to her slippers, purposely nudging her foot a little. She didn't notice.

"Game's on," he said.

She nodded without looking up.

He tried again. "Looks like it's a good one. Top of the fourth, Dodgers ahead six to two."

"Great," she said absently.

How could she read that stuff when there was a game on? Glancing at her absorbed face, Jake slapped his thigh loudly as the catcher missed the pitch.

Amy kept reading.

He groaned noisily as the runner was thrown out at home.

She turned the page.

He whooped as the batter swung at the umpire.

She read on. Suddenly, she chuckled.

"How can I concentrate on the game with you making so much racket!" Jake exploded. "Haven't you memorized that book by now? You read it often enough."

"What?" Startled by his outburst Amy sat up a little, blinking at him. "Oh. Sorry."

To his surprise, a blush crept under her smooth skin, settling high on her cheekbones. Averting her gaze, she set the book on her lap. She grabbed a handful of popcorn and focused on the TV. "Good game, isn't it?"

Jake stared at her. "Yeah. Riveting." He took some popcorn and tossed the fluffy kernels into his mouth. Chewing, he watched the game a second, then swallowed. "So, what part were you reading?" Casually, he stretched his hand toward the book.

Just as casually, Amy moved it out of his reach, placing it on her other side. "Oh, something about courtship stages. Would you like some more popcorn?"

"No, thanks." He yawned, feigning disinterest. "So, what do you mean, courtship stages?"

Amy shrugged. "Stages successful marriages go through during courtship, that's all." She gestured at the television and watched intently. "Look who's coming up to bat."

Jake didn't bother; his gaze stayed fixed on Amy. "Yeah. Are you saying that in order to have a successful marriage, a couple has to go through a set of courtship stages?"

Amy set the popcorn bowl on the coffee table, and slouched down, crossing her arms over her chest. "*I'm* not saying anything. Dr. Potocki merely mentions that the majority of couples with successful marriages all progressed through similar stages in their courtship."

"They do?"

"That's what it says."

Jake waited, but she didn't elaborate. Impatiently, he prompted, "Such as?"

Amy sighed. "Such as, hand to hand contact, then hand to shoulder, and so on."

He raised his brow. "So on?"

"Jake, are you interested in the game or not?"

"Sure." He watched the batter take a sucker pitch and hit it to the second baseman who threw him out at first for the end of the inning. He shifted a little closer to Amy, camouflaging the move by stretching elaborately.

He waited patiently until Amy picked up the book again, then pounced. Ignoring her shrieks, he used his weight to hold her down while he caught both of her wrists in one hand.

Amy arched up to try to oust him from the couch. Unfortunately, Jake was too big to be easily oustable. His grip on her wrists remained firmly secure. Her bucking movement merely lifted her sweatshirt, allowing his hard forearm to press against her bare stomach. Uncomfortably aware of the friction caused by his hairy arm rubbing against her bare skin, she lay still.

Reaching over, he plucked the book away from her. "Got it!" He sat down again at his end of the couch.

Her face flushed, Amy gritted her teeth. "Give me the book, Jake."

He smiled with mocking satisfaction. "No."

"You...you..." Infuriated, she tried to grab it, but he was too quick. "Why are you so interested, anyway?" she demanded, puffing so her bangs flew up out of her eyes.

"Why not? I might decide to get married someday." Her expression was clearly skeptical. Disregarding it, he asked, "Why are *you* so determined that I don't read it?"

She folded her arms. "Go ahead. Never mind that I was reading it first."

"Thanks." Ignoring her sarcastic tone, Jake turned off the sound on the television with the remote control and opened the book. He scanned the table of contents, then flipped to the chapter titled "Ensuring a Successful Marriage." "Ah, here we go. 'In most successful marriages, the couples progressed through startlingly similar courtship stages. Since intimacy is built slowly, couples who skip these stages are more apt to experience difficulties later in their marriage.' Whew! Heavy stuff," he said to Amy's unresponsive profile.

She crossed her legs, swinging her feet so the bunnies' heads repeatedly knocked together.

After a wary glance at the slippers, Jake continued, " 'First the couples experience hand to hand contact, then hand to shoulder, hand to mouth, mouth to mouth, hand to breast'... I knew this would get more interesting...'mouth to breast, and sexual intercourse.' " He paused, then stared at her. "That's it?"

"Of course that's it." Annoyed, Amy jerked her book out of his grasp. "What did you expect?"

"I don't know. Something more involved than that. Seems to me they missed a few areas along the way." Reaching down, he pulled her feet off the table, settling them onto his lap. His finger and thumb encircled her slim ankle. "What about hand to foot contact?" Gently, he rubbed his thumb over the delicate skin covering her anklebone.

She tried to pull her foot away, but Jake wouldn't let her, firmly holding her feet still. Amy swallowed.

"What about it?" Her sweatshirt had pulled up revealing her shorts, and uneasily, she pushed it back down over her thighs.

"I think it's an important stage. Don't you?"

"Of course not." Silently though, Amy conceded he might have a point. Jake's calloused fingers on her skin triggered a current of sexual awareness that sizzled up the inside of her legs to burn at the top of her cutoffs.

He's only holding your feet—hardly an X-rated action, she told herself. It'd be silly to fuss about it. What could she say—*unhand my foot, you cad?* She comforted herself with the thought that he probably didn't realize the effect he was having on her.

He removed her slippers, brushing his thumb along her sole. Amy shivered. He'd never touched her feet before. Come to think of it, no man had. In a way, she supposed her feet were kind of…virgin territory. Like the rest of her. Jake began a circling massage on the bottom of her foot. She closed her eyes for a moment in helpless enjoyment. Why had she waited twenty-four years to discover this aching pleasure?

Jake's voice, strangely husky, wandered into her hedonistic daydream. "You have beautiful feet."

Without opening her eyes, Amy replied, "You once said my toes looked like Fred Flintstone's."

Jake smiled a little. Short, squared, almost all the same size, they did resemble the cartoon caveman's. Amy's though, were much cuter. "I couldn't have," he answered solemnly. "Fred would never wear pink polish."

Fred didn't have such shapely ankles and calves, either. Jake slid his hand a little higher, exploring the sensitive area behind her knees.

He didn't intend to let things go too far; he'd never consciously do anything to hurt Amy. But damn it, she needed to stop thinking of him as a nonsexual being. *Why* this had become so imperative, he shied away from answering.

He stroked her smooth tanned legs. A spark of awareness between them wouldn't spoil their friendship, he assured himself. Hell, he knew better than to let things get out of hand. But right now, he couldn't seem to stop touching her. His fingers trailed up along her soft inner thigh.

His fingers slipped under the material of her shorts. Amy's eyes fluttered open. Jake froze, then tiptoed his fingers down again to her ankles. He shifted her bare feet in his lap.

Amy exhaled the breath she'd been holding, and relaxed. She sent Jake a questioning glance.

He avoided it by picking up her hand, which lay on the couch between them. "Hand to hand contact is first, hmm? Yeah, I can see where that would be important," he said.

He turned her hand over, testing the resiliency of her small palm. He pressed the center with his thumb, and her fingers curled reflexively. With his finger he traced and outlined her hand then gently caressed the sensitive skin between each finger. Amy's eyes, which had drooped half-shut again, shot open as he slid one of her fingers in his mouth and suckled it.

She stared at him. He *was* coming on to her—no doubt about it. The problem was, she didn't think she wanted him to stop. Her hand looked white and fragile next to the hard, brown planes of his face. His eyes, meeting hers, had darkened to a smoky gray. Amy began trembling as each tug of his mouth on her finger tightened a hard knot of desire in the bottom of her stomach. Unable to stand anymore, she yanked her hand away. Sitting up, she clasped her hands safely together in her lap, drawing her legs away from him.

Jake didn't let her escape that easily. Her eyes widened when he moved closer and slipped an arm around her. "Hand to shoulder next, wasn't it?" he said huskily. He pulled her gently across his lap, supporting her shoulders with his arm.

She began to sit up from her semireclining position. "Jake?"

He didn't answer her confused protest. Threading his fingers through her hair, he repeatedly combed the clinging curls as she looked up at him.

Slowly, her eyes drifted closed. She should get up, move away from Jake and the unexpected temptation he was offering. But the stroking motion of his hand was so soothing, so comforting, her willpower seemed to seep away with his touch.

Jake hadn't noticed the sun finally setting, but the silent television splattered muted colors around the darkened room, highlighting the creamy yellow of Amy's sweatshirt, the hint of rose in her cheeks. He rubbed his chin against her hair, tightening his arms around her. He breathed deeply. Her lemony shampoo provided a tart contrast to the fresh, sweet scent that was Amy's alone.

Lifting his head, Jake studied her face as the light alternately concealed and revealed her expression. Her lips bowed in a sensual curve, her dark lashes fanned her cheeks.

He bent and touched her soft mouth with his own. Sweet...oh, so sweet. He couldn't remember ever wondering about kissing Amy, yet somehow she tasted like he knew she would. Sweeter than strawberries dipped in cream. She tasted like contentment, like fulfillment. She tasted like Amy.

He nuzzled her neck and discovered the sensitive spot behind her ear that made her shiver. He nipped her lobe, then trailed a row of kisses along her delicate jaw back to her mouth.

Then her lips parted and contentment ebbed away. Need swept over him. His tongue swirled in to claim hers on a rising tide of desire. Crushing her mouth beneath his, his body hardened as hers softened against him. Control slipped.

Amy gasped as his strong arms squeezed her until she lost her breath. His hold immediately loosened and she linked her arms around his neck, gripping him tighter. She didn't need air; she needed Jake as close as she could get him.

She broke the kiss and nuzzled his muscled neck, inhaling scents of soap and man overlaid with the spicy smell of sawdust she always associated with Jake. She pressed her mouth to the warm hollow beneath his throat. His pulse beat quickened and he groaned, the deep sound vibrating against her lips.

Jake swept his hand over her thighs and cutoffs. Drowning in sensation, he burrowed under her sweatshirt, exploring her flat stomach, feeling her muscles contract as his callused palm roved over her. He reached upward to cover her breast. Her nipple thrust against her cotton bra, and he gently pressed it with his thumb. He felt Amy quiver in reaction.

Eager to touch her bare skin, he tried to slide his hand beneath her bra. The elastic was too stiff. Reaching behind her, he fumbled with the clasp a moment. Finally, he rasped in her ear, "Sit up, babe, so I can open this," and eased her to a sitting position with her back to him.

Amy's head lolled lazily. Blinking, she opened her eyes. Bereft of Jake's warmth, the sensual haze surrounding her began to dissipate. When he lifted the back of her sweatshirt and the cool breeze flowed against her heated skin, the haze cleared completely.

What on earth were they doing?

Budding panic edged out the sexual need she'd felt moments before. She was on the verge of making love—*no, call it what it is, Amy*—on the verge of having sex with Jake!

She gasped as her bra fell forward. Crossing her arms to hold it in place beneath her shirt, she scooted away from him to the end of the couch. She was trembling uncontrollably; partly from the sudden, almost unbearable cessation of their lovemaking, but even more from fear. Fear of losing Jake.

Feeling exposed and vulnerable, she wrapped her arms around herself. How stupid to begin something that she didn't dare to complete. Love, desire, lust— call it what you would—were fleeting emotions, not to be counted on in the practical reality of daily living. Hadn't her parents taught her that? Never had two people been so mismatched as her coldly, analytical father and her foolishly affectionate mother. Once their blind passion had burnt itself out, the only emotions left to fill the void were bitterness and regret which spilled into their every conversation.

Pain filled her at the memory, and Amy pressed her shaky hands to her hot cheeks. If it hadn't been for Maddie and Jake... How could she jeopardize the only stable relationships in her life? Love didn't last, friendship did. Did she really want to gamble with Jake's friendship?

"What's wrong, sweetheart?"

Amy's throat constricted at his deeply possessive tone. She shivered, crossing her arms as she glanced at him. Half-shadowed, half-illuminated, his rugged face looked strangely unfamiliar. Stark passion glazed his eyes, altering his features into a tight mask that almost frightened her. Never had he looked at her like that before. Amy stilled, as an unwelcome thought crept into her mind. Was he seeing *her,* Amy, or was this the way he looked at any willing woman? She didn't intend to voice the thought, but somehow the words escaped into the quiet room. "Do you know what you're doing, Jake?"

About to gather her back into his arms, Jake paused. Amy was huddled at the end of the couch, with her crossed arms shielding her chest. Her lips were still swollen from his kisses, her eyes dilated with newly awakened sexual desire. But the sleepy sensuality in her expression was rapidly being replaced with suspicion.

Studying her face, Jake felt growing rage expanding in his chest. Leaning back, he folded his arms. "Are you asking for references?"

Amy stiffened. "Of course not. I'm asking if you realize who you're making love to."

"Maybe you should be asking yourself that question, Amy," he said dryly. "I've been here before. Not with as many women as you probably imagine, yet enough to know if I don't know who's in my arms, then it isn't worth it. What about you?"

She said slowly, "If you're asking if I ever—"

"No, I'm not. I *know* you've never." He gave a harsh laugh. "Hell, you're so afraid of love you've concocted a harebrained scheme to avoid it."

"That's not true!" She rose on shaky legs.

Jake stood up, too, looming over her. "Didn't you stop because you suddenly remembered who I am?" he demanded fiercely. "Or rather who I'm *not?* I'm *not* one of your stereotyped marriage candidates, Amy. And the sooner you realize that, the better it will be for both of us. Which brings us back to your original question: do *you* know what you're doing?"

She tried to speak; her throat seemed to be clogged. She cleared it and managed to choke out, "You're right. You're not my idea of an ideal husband. Which means we're destroying a perfectly good friendship for nothing."

At her words pain lanced through Jake's stomach. He tensed, his hands on his hips. "Is that how you see it? That we're destroying our friendship?"

She nodded. "Isn't it true? We've disagreed, but we've never fought like this before." Images of her parents' bitter arguments flickered through her mind. "Sex is messing things up already."

He didn't respond, and she looked at him solemnly. "What do you want from me, Jake? Isn't friendship enough?"

His gazed probed hers. "Is it enough for you?"

She bit her lip, then nodded. "Yes."

"Then I guess it's enough for me, too."

Anxious to escape to her room, Amy hesitated. There was a strange note in his voice she didn't understand. Maybe he was regretting having her live here. Her throat tightened but she forced herself to offer, "If my staying here is going to be a problem, I can find another place."

Jake turned away. "No need to do that," he said casually over his shoulder. He picked up the remote control from the table, then sat back on the couch. He glanced up at her, his gray eyes indifferent. "Unless it's a problem for you?"

"No."

"Fine." He looked at the TV screen. "So we'll forget tonight ever happened and go back to being just good friends." He added emphatically, *"No problem."*

Chapter Seven

He had a problem.

Jake stared expressionlessly at the pancakes in front of him. The pile towered at least six inches high, each flat golden cake a symmetrical circle overlapping the edges of the plate. Two melting squares of butter floated on the top.

Jake loved pancakes. Usually. On a typical day he would have finished off this batch and devoured two more like it before even considering leaving the table. However, this wasn't a typical day. Every move Amy made as she bustled around the kitchen reminded him of that fact.

"Hungry?" she asked, pausing by his chair a moment.

"Starved," he answered, forcing enthusiasm into his voice.

She moved away again when he picked up the pitcher, tilting it so maple syrup oozed out over the stack. He watched her from the corner of his eye.

Most mornings Amy came downstairs still in a sleepy stupor. Her hair spiking out in all directions, wearing her old robe and cotton pajamas, she'd silently fix his breakfast with instinctive efficiency between jaw-breaking yawns.

Today, however, she was fully dressed in tennis shoes, socks, jeans and a white blouse, topped by a bright pink sweatshirt. In August. With the temperature already hitting eighty degrees at seven in the morning, and heading for the nineties.

His stomach roiling, Jake wondered if she'd piled on the layers of clothes as protection against him. Surely, she didn't think he would try and force her into anything she didn't want to do. The lady had a right to say no. He'd planned to talk to her about last night, but after a quick glance at his face, Amy had become oh-so-busy. Obviously, she wanted to forget the whole incident. She certainly wasn't going to give him a chance to discuss anything personal. Fine by him.

He wasn't exactly sure what he'd say, anyway. Last night he'd been too overwhelmed by the scent, sound and feel of Amy in his arms to think clearly. This morning, surprise and guilt helped tamp down his stirring libido.

To begin with, Amy was looking for a husband; he wasn't interested in a wife. And kids? Jake tried to imagine having a houseful of children. He shuddered and picked up his coffee cup for a sip. The picture was not an appealing one.

Although—he paused, slanting a glance at Amy's slim figure as she washed out a frying pan—he did feel a certain warmth deep in his chest at the thought of her carrying his child. But did he want the responsibility of a family? Maddie was his family, and she provided plenty of aggravation alone.

At the thought of his grandmother, he winced. And wouldn't Maddie be pleased if she learned that her dear grandson had tried to seduce her innocent young friend? He doubted Amy would tell her; he certainly wouldn't. He wasn't intimidated by too many people anymore; he'd learned to stand up for himself against hard-nosed business or construction men by the time he was twenty-five. He'd also learned he'd rather face a dozen bloodthirsty bricklayers than his grandmother when she was angry.

He looked up as Amy said suddenly, "After I finish the grocery shopping, I'm going to drive over and check out the shops on Balboa Island. Maybe I'll get up the courage to get my ears pierced. Harvey says it makes a big improvement in a woman's appearance."

Sensing she was waiting for a comment, Jake grunted an assent. Her tone sounded calm, friendly. *She* didn't seem to be having second thoughts about stopping last night. To her, they were back to being old friends.

He picked up his fork, ignoring the rumbling protests his stomach made at the action. Fine with him. Grimly, he began slicing through the mountain of pancakes. The more he considered it, that was the best way to handle the whole situation. He forced himself to swallow the mouthful he'd been chewing for the past two minutes. The gooey mess slid slowly down his throat, lodged for a moment and then, thankfully, continued on its way.

Jake speared another forkful. He had no problem just being friends. No problem at all.

"...Next time I go out, I think I'll keep it more low-key. Just a quiet restaurant—"

"You're still looking for a husband?" He hadn't meant to sound so abrupt. He watched Amy's back stiffen as she paused in her scrubbing of the white porcelain stove. Looking over her shoulder, she met his eyes. For a fleeting second, he thought he glimpsed uncertainty, but before he could interpret her expression, it was gone, replaced by a quick bright smile as she turned back to her project.

"Sure I'm going to continue. Why wouldn't I? Of course, I realize now that it wasn't fair of me to involve you in my plans. I'll meet someone eventually. The book recommends several places where singles gather. I thought I might try the beach."

Not the beach, Jake decided. Not in those two neon green scraps she'd pulled out of a shopping bag and called a bikini.

"So please don't worry anymore—"

Don't worry? When she was planning to parade the beach practically naked? He abandoned the pancakes and picked up his coffee. "I said I'd help you and I will."

"But you're so busy at work, I realize—"

"In fact," he cut in, "I have another date lined up for you already. It slipped my mind, but I'll have the guy call you this afternoon. Okay by you?"

"Wonderful!"

Yeah. Wonderful. Now all he had to do was choose a man he could trust and convince him to go out with Amy. He frowned when no one came to mind. At least he had a few hours to find someone. Scowling, he put down his coffee and headed for the door.

Amy managed to keep her smile on her face until the front door slammed. Then the smile wobbled a little, but determinedly she pasted it back on.

Jake had apparently put their lovemaking entirely out of his mind, while she'd tossed and turned reliving every minute, wondering if she'd made the right choice. She knew now she had. It was true what her mother and the book had warned her about: a man's desire was too fleeting to base a relationship on.

Even Maddie had mentioned once the pitfall of giving in to lust. "Darling, so many foolish women these days give their hearts, as well as their bodies, before they even know if the man is interested in marriage. They're just asking to be hurt!"

Well, she wasn't. Maddie was right, and Jake was a perfect example. He hadn't once brought up what had happened; he'd forgotten all about it. He already had a date planned for her. Great! Just what she wanted to hear.

Bless his big old black heart.

When Jake came home that evening, Amy was careful to treat him as though the previous night had never happened. Which wasn't difficult, she thought wryly, since he hardly noticed her as he walked around with a preoccupied frown on his face after telling her he'd set up the date.

Shorty arrived the following night. After Jake introduced them, he went into the kitchen for drinks. Amy excused herself to follow, leaving Shorty sitting on the couch nervously cracking his knuckles.

"What's the idea, Jake," she demanded as soon as the kitchen door swung shut behind her.

"Huh?" He glanced at her around the open cupboard door.

"What's the idea with Shorty?"

"He's your date."

"I know he's my date. But the man is wearing an orange shirt, red tie and brown suit. Don't tell me he always dresses like that."

"No, that's the outfit he wears for special occasions." Jake selected a couple of glasses and set them on the counter.

"You mean you didn't tell him to dress like that as a joke?"

Jake looked surprised. "Would I do something like that?" Amy stared at him steadily. "Okay, maybe I would, but I didn't. It happens that Shorty is a little color blind."

"Oh." Amy bit her lip. Color blind—that put a different perspective on things. For some reason, she felt a little disappointed. It wasn't that she was expecting Jake to sabotage her plan. Still, why did she keep ending up with such *unusual* dates? "Was he the only one you could find?"

Leaning back against the counter, Jake crossed his arms in front of his chest. "No, but Shorty fits your specifications completely. He's twenty-seven. He's not tall, dark or handsome. He loves children. He's very neat—at least on the job. I've never seen him act violently, and he's got a great sense of humor." He lowered his voice, adding confidentially, "Once he did this great imitation of a pimple. He put a Twinkie in his mouth and then—"

"Thank you," Amy interrupted. "My fourteen-year-old students do that same imitation. I get the picture."

"You did ask." A grin tugged at the corner of his straight lips, but he suppressed it. "What's the problem with Shorty, Amy? Are you starting to realize that maybe marriage isn't an answer? Especially when you aren't attracted to a man, a man you'd be living, eating and *sleeping* with for the rest of your life? Is your goal, by any chance, changing?" He stood up, taking a step toward her.

Amy moved back, bumping into the counter. "No, it's not. I believe in marriage. The important thing is to have a man with the same values, like wanting children, a family. *Sleeping,* as you so delicately put it, is only a small part of a marriage relationship."

Jake raised his eyebrows. "Are you ever misinformed," he said dryly.

Amy compressed her lips.

His gaze fastened on her stubborn mouth, then drifted down over her blue dress to her matching spike heels. He reached up to gently grasp her shoulders, his callused fingertips rasping over the silk. He tilted her chin up to look into her face. "Can I make a suggestion?" he said softly, his warm breath stirring the curls at her temple.

Amy's annoyance melted as a wave of heat traveled from her tummy to her breasts. Involuntarily, her lips parted slightly. Jake's firm mouth was so close to her own. "What?"

He leaned a little closer. "Don't wear the heels with Shorty." His white teeth suddenly gleamed in a mocking grin. He dropped his hands and turned back to the counter.

Amy blinked. "Oh. Right." Face flushed, she headed for the stairs to change into her flat white sandals.

Less than fifteen minutes later, Amy maneuvered Shorty out of the house and away from Jake's disturbing presence. She was determined to enjoy the evening, and one of the best ways to do that was not to give Jake another thought, but concentrate on her date.

Shorty's height made a pleasant change, Amy told herself firmly, as she preceded him down the walk to his blue sedan. Tall, handsome men—like Jake—were too often shallow, overly confident and aggravating. Shorty's shortness made him special: there weren't too many men she could look directly in the eye.

Not that Shorty had yet looked her in the eye. The man apparently was either shy or very quiet. Politely, he opened her car door, the action causing his face to flush a deep red, only a shade or two lighter than his tie, Amy noticed. On the way to the Crab Cooker every topic of conversation she tried to initiate reproduced the blush that soon became as painful to her as it apparently was to Shorty. She felt a surge of gratitude when the gaudy red building with the green awnings came into view.

Once a bank, the forty-one-year-old restaurant was a landmark in the beach community. Behind its market counter, where take-out orders were handled, was a big walk-in cooler that had once been a vault. Gradually, the casual, sea-themed decor at the restaurant seemed to have a beneficial effect on Shorty. He became more talkative as they discussed the merits of the restaurant's famous smoked albacore and Manhattan-style clam chowder. And when she inadvertently hit on the topic closest to his heart—tilework—shy Shorty grabbed the conversational ball and took off, leaving her with nothing to do but push her salad around her plate and smile or nod at intervals.

"Yes, the color of the grout between the tiles makes all the difference," Shorty said. "A popular color right now is silver-gray, since it goes with..."

Jake's eyes were silver-gray. Amy ran a finger around the bowl of her plastic spoon. When he teased her, they sparkled like polished silver. They'd been the color of pewter tonight, and for one second, she thought he'd been about to kiss her. The terrible part was, although she knew what a mistake it would be, she'd wanted him to. She'd wanted to feel again the piercing excitement only Jake had made her feel.

"... Setting the tile is where you have to be extra careful..."

She had to be more careful. Careful not to tease him, not to stay in the same room too long, not to touch. He was being careful, too. Tonight was the first time he'd even come close to her in the past two days. Oh, how she missed touching Jake—those casual, affectionate hugs that for years she'd taken for granted.

"... Yep, even when that expensive box of Italian tiles turned up cracked, the boss never blamed us. Jake, he plays fair with his men..."

Yes, he did play fair. Jake wouldn't take the easy way out. He'd been up-front with his feelings about marriage, right from the beginning. He wanted her, but how long would that last? He already seemed to have put her out of his mind. Yet, she'd swear she'd glimpsed desire simmering occasionally in his eyes, felt tension between them.

"Jake sure is one in a million..."

Yes, he was. One man with seven million single women to choose from, to be exact. There was no one like Jake. No one could make her laugh, comfort her, or make her ache with desire like Jake Joseph Weston. But no one else could ever make her as angry or hurt her as much, either. He could send her soaring to emotional heights she'd never dreamed of, but he could also send her crashing down to earth. The intensity of the emotions he aroused frightened her. She wasn't looking for raging passion; she wanted a calm, level-headed type of relationship. Jake—even if he was ready for marriage—was definitely not her type.

"...So there's something I want to share about my feelings for you."

Amy's head jerked up and her spoon fell to the tile floor. Apparently, she'd missed an important part of the conversation. Shorty was moving *much* too fast. She took a deep breath and opened her mouth to gently set him straight. She needed to make it clear that—

"Although you are a very nice person, there can never be anything between us."

Amy's mouth snapped shut. The words were hers, but strangely enough they came from Shorty.

He continued, "I wouldn't want to lead you on, or anything. Jake asked me to take you to dinner, and shoot, I'd do anything for Jake." His voice dropped sympathetically. "He told me how you never get out."

Amy's lips pursed. *Thank you, Jake.*

"Besides, anything is better than moping around my apartment another evening..."

Her lips tightened more. *And thank you, Shorty.*

Shorty must have read something of her reaction in her expression because he added hastily, "Not that I think you're interested in me. It's just, well, I like to be honest." His face the color of the empty lobster shell on his plate, he stumbled on. "You see, I'm in love with someone else. I have been for years. I hope you understand."

He was obviously sincere. The poor man looked ready to crawl under his chair. Amy sighed. Chalk off another husband prospect. "Of course I understand." She frowned, stirring her coffee thoughtfully. "But isn't your girlfriend going to be angry that you're out with me?"

"I wish." Shorty slouched back in his chair. "Sue doesn't know I love her. We've been dating for six months and I was working up the courage to ask her to marry me. Then it happened."

He broke off with such a look of suffering on his face that Amy felt a surge of sympathy. She leaned across the red tabletop. "Then what happened, Shorty?"

He sighed, his blue eyes full of misery. "She lost weight."

Amy sat back abruptly. "That's it? She lost weight?" She felt bewildered. "What's wrong with that? I'd think you'd be proud of her. Don't you think she looks attractive?"

"Oh, yeah. She looks great."

Amy was nonplussed. "So what's the problem?"

Shorty ran his hand through his hair. "You don't understand. Sue lost more than *fifty pounds*. She was beautiful before, but now she's a knockout. She looks so good that whenever we went out, people would stare at us like they were thinking, 'What's a gorgeous woman like that doing with such an ugly guy?' Who can blame them?"

He gave a rueful chuckle. "She told me it wasn't true, that she thought I was great, but I know she deserves someone better. By now, she's probably glad I quit calling her. After all, I'm not exactly Mr. America. Look at me."

For the first time, Amy really looked at the man across from her. His red hair seemed electrified, bursting in curly clumps around his head, and, okay, his clothes sense *was* atrocious. Still, his blue eyes were gentle and his good humor was evident in the smile lines etched on his round face.

Jake was right—Shorty did fit her listed specifications, and whether he knew it or not, he probably fulfilled those of his ex-girlfriend Sue. It sounded like she hadn't wanted to break up, that it was all Shorty's idea. If it wasn't for his lack of confidence...but then, who knew better than her the difference it made to your self-esteem to know you looked your best. Why, if it wasn't for Harvey—

She snapped her fingers. "That's it! Harvey will change your image."

Over skewered shrimp, she elaborated on her idea. After his first reservations subsided, Shorty's enthusiasm soon surpassed her own.

"You promise you'll go with me tomorrow to see this Harvey guy?" he asked for at least the fifth time between bites of cod. "I've never been in a hair salon before. Seems kind of sissy to me. I go to the barber."

"Hair salons are no longer considered sissy," Amy answered firmly. If Harvey heard a remark like that, he'd probably dye Shorty's hair purple.

Shorty took a deep breath. "I'll do it. If I want a girl like Sue, I need to have the courage to go after her."

Amy smiled at Shorty, feeling bolstered by his resolve. Maybe she needed to reevaluate her plan, too. She needed to take control, stop being a coward and find a husband, with or without Jake's help. She put down her coffee cup decisively. If Shorty could put aside his fears, then so could she.

"I'll definitely go to Harvey's with you," she told Shorty. "It's time I made some changes, too. For a start, I will get my ears pierced." She pushed the thought of needles, blood and pain away and held up her paper cup.

Shorty bumped his solemnly against it.

Amy put down her cup. She savored a bit of shrimp and glanced across the table. "Are you positive Jake will let you have the day off?"

Shorty nodded. "Sure. I have time coming. I'll just give Rosie a call in the morning and let her know our plans, and that I probably won't be in until later." He finished his coffee and signaled the waiter for the check.

Amy put her fork down, surveying her empty plate regretfully. For the first time in two days she'd managed to forget the situation with Jake long enough to enjoy a meal. She hated for the evening to end.

Shorty must have felt the same. He said hesitantly, "Say, Amy, it's only nine o'clock. How 'bout we catch the latest *Rocky* movie?"

Rocky. Just the thing to build a fighting mood. Amy grinned and pushed back her chair. "Let's go!"

Chapter Eight

Jake tilted back in his chair the next morning and scowled at the clock on his office wall. Nine o'clock and no Shorty. Throwing down his pen, he stalked to the door and yanked it open.

Rosie, seated behind an oak desk that was even more massive than his own, glanced up briefly then looked back down at her typing. As usual, she had on the bright purple suit she'd worn every Friday since she'd been hired. She reminded Jake of an animated grape—a plump, *sour* grape—as she ignored him and pegged away at the forty-year-old black typewriter she adamantly refused to abandon.

"Rosie—"

"Don't do it, Jake." Her typing continued uninterrupted, but he could see her lips tighten into a thin line.

He paused, one shoulder braced in the doorway. "Don't do what?"

Rosie slapped at the slender carriage return and the machine emitted a loud "ping." "Don't ask me again what Shorty said." Ping! "I've told you three times that he called in to say he'd be late." Ping! "He said that Amy and he are tired of being cowards, that they're going to do something about it." Ping! "And for the last time, I don't *know* what he meant by that, he hung up before I could ask." Ping! Ping! Ping!

"How on earth could you let him get off the phone after a message like that?" Jake scowled, crossing his arms.

"I didn't *let* him. He hung up."

Jake frowned again. "Well, what in the hell did he mean?"

Deliberately, Rosie lifted her hands from the keys and fixed him with a cold stare. "I told you I have no idea. I gave up understanding irrational men at eight o'clock this morning when you stormed in."

Jake looked up at the ceiling for patience. "I try to make sense out of a ridiculous, asinine message, and I'm called irrational! Women!" Turning, he stalked back into his office, slamming the door.

He immediately opened it again and stuck his head out. "Shorty sounded pleased?"

Rosie sighed. "Yes."

"Would you say he sounded happy?"

"Yes."

"Exactly how happy?"

"Ecstatic! He sounded ecstatic!" She reared up, planting her fists on her desk as she leaned forward threateningly. "But not half as ecstatic as I'm going to feel when you finally *leave me alone!*"

Jake slammed the door again, resisting the urge to give it a solid kick. Damn! Nothing was going as he'd anticipated—which was what he should have anticipated when it came to Amy.

He dropped back down in his chair and wearily leaned back his head. What was going on?

Last night, he'd been pleased by Amy's reaction to Shorty when she first saw him in his orange shirt and red tie. He'd hoped it was finally getting through to her that using a book to find a husband wasn't going to work. Did she honestly believe she could marry a man she wasn't attracted to; that lust and love were incompatible? He hoped not, because he was almost positive Amy was "in lust" with him. Last night when he'd crowded her in the kitchen, for a moment he'd sworn her eyes had the same drowsy look they'd had when he'd kissed her before.

It'd been hard to step away. It was harder yet watching her leave with Shorty in that blue dress that delineated each curve of her breasts and bottom. If she'd been going with anyone but Shorty, he would've been pacing the floor all night. But Shorty had admitted he was carrying a torch for Sue. If Jake hadn't portrayed Amy as a lonely, lost soul and stirred Shorty's soft heart, he wouldn't have been able to get him to agree to go out with her at all.

Jake frowned. And that was another problem. Knowing that Shorty hadn't been anxious to go out with her, he'd fallen asleep on the couch waiting for them to get home. He never heard Amy come in, and she wasn't stirring when he'd opened the stairwell door this morning to listen. He'd waited until the last possible minute to leave for work, slamming pots and pans around as loudly as possible, but no Amy.

A thought began to niggle at the back of his mind. Had she even come home? He immediately rejected the unwelcome idea. Of course she had.

But what had Shorty meant about being cowards, and doing something about it? Amy wasn't a coward. The only thing he could think that she might be afraid of was making love.

Jake straightened suddenly in his chair. She wouldn't—would she?

He slumped back, crossing his arms. The idea was not only obscene, it was ludicrous. Shorty loved Sue. He had for years.

Jake shifted uncomfortably, rubbing the tight muscles in his neck. But Amy *had* looked damn sexy last night. And they were spending the day together. Had she slept with him?

Damn it, no. He relaxed slightly, propping his work boots up on the desk and linking his arms behind his head. Amy wasn't promiscuous; hell *he* knew that. Besides, she'd just met Shorty—there's no way she'd spend the night with him, even if he did fit the requirements on her list. She wasn't attracted to Shorty. He'd swear she wasn't.

Amy wasn't looking for desire. In fact, it frightened her. Ironically, she'd probably feel safer making love with someone she *didn't* desire. His feet dropped to the floor with a thud.

Someone like Shorty.

Jake's stomach constricted at the thought. Would the risk seem less to her with Shorty? Had she decided to finally jump in with both feet and become involved? After all, whether she faced it or not she was scared of emotional entanglements. Surely, she wouldn't have . . .

Jake snorted. This was ridiculous. He pulled the payroll across the desk toward him, determined to forget these ridiculous ideas and get some work done. Hell, he sure hadn't put in his usual time these past couple of weeks.

Time. What time *had* she come in? Surely he would have heard Shorty's car. And as for Shorty, exactly how ecstatic had Rosie said he'd been?

Frowning, he absentmindedly stood up and headed back into Rosie's office. She looked up with a long-suffering sigh.

"You again?"

The phone rang, and Rosie reached for it at the same time Jake lunged across her desk. Rosie won. With her hand on the receiver, her expression dared him to try and take it away. Impatiently he backed off. With a triumphant smile, she greeted the caller.

"Hello? Oh, hello, Amy."

Jake's hand shot out in a demanding gesture. Rosie ignored it. "How are you today? How nice. Fine, thank you. Yes, I think Jake is in. Just a minute."

Covering the receiver with her hand, she looked up at him. "It's Amy."

Jake glared back. "No kidding." He started to take the receiver, glanced at Rosie's carefully impassive expression, and changed his mind. "I'll take it in my office." He walked nonchalantly into his office and shut the door quietly behind him. His chair swiveled as he grabbed the phone. "Amy?"

"Just a minute please," Rosie's voice responded.

Jake heard a click and Amy's voice traveled over the line. "Jake? Thank goodness you're there. Did Shorty call?"

"Earlier, but—"

"Then you know. Oh, Jake, I think I made a big mistake."

Jake's stomach tightened. Was she crying? Something was wrong. "Amy, are you all right?"

"Of course, I'm all right. I was just so scared." She sniffed defensively. "I know that sounds stupid, but it *did* hurt. Everyone always said there's just a little pain, and some women have told me they didn't feel any at all." Her voice lowered. "I swear, Jake, I almost screamed."

Jake leaned over his desk, covering his eyes with his hand. Years ago, he'd slipped and fallen off a one-story roof. For a moment he felt again the same dizzy, disoriented feeling followed by thudding pain.

His fears were true: Amy had given up her virginity. To a virtual stranger.

He'd thought he was liberated. Liberated, hell, he didn't even feel civilized. Rage burned through him, and he said tersely, "I'm going to kill Shorty."

Amy's voice sounded stronger. "You can't blame Shorty. It was my idea. I was tired of being a coward. I thought it would make me more attractive and sophisticated. Really, he tried to talk me out of it, but I wouldn't listen."

Jake swallowed. "Amy, you were fine the way you were. How could you believe something like that? Especially after waiting all these years?"

"If you're trying to make me feel better, you aren't doing a very good job. It's a little late now."

Jake sighed. Wearily, he rubbed the back of his head. She was right. Still, he couldn't resist saying, "Babe, if you were determined to... do it, why didn't you come to me instead of a stranger?"

There was silence. "To be honest, Jake, I never even thought about asking you."

He closed his eyes. After all they'd shared through the years and in spite of the other night, she hadn't thought of him. Mingled anger and hurt constricted his chest in a giant band of pain.

Amy continued, "Besides, I wanted someone who was experienced and knew what they were doing."

Jake opened his eyes again. Anger drowned the pain. *Experience* hadn't been on her list. He started to say so when she added, her voice sounding puzzled, "I never realized you'd even want to."

He gave the receiver a disbelieving look. He'd *thought* he'd made his wishes clear the other night. True, he hadn't specifically said he wanted to make love, and they'd avoided the issue since. If Amy needed to hear the words, he'd say them now here and avoid any further misunderstanding. "I did, babe." His voice sounded husky. He cleared his throat. "I still do."

"Oh." She paused. "Well, I suppose if I ever get up the courage to do it again..."

She sounded doubtful, and he said, "You will, Amy. I'm sure of it. And when you're with someone you care about, instead of a stranger like Shorty—"

"Shorty! Is that what you thought?" Amy gave a relieved laugh. "Shorty didn't do it. Harvey did!"

"What!"

"I said, Harvey—remember my hairdresser? He did it with a gun."

"A gun!"

"Yes. He pierced my ears with a gun." She chuckled. "Didn't you know they use a gun? I suppose you thought they still used a needle?"

She waited, but Jake, battling waves of surprise, anger and overwhelming relief, didn't answer—couldn't answer. *All this agony was for pierced ears?*

Would he *never* learn?

When he remained silent, Amy continued, "How could you think I'd trust Shorty to pierce my ears? Of course, I'd ask you before Shorty. Why, he almost fainted when Harvey did my second ear."

Jake felt a little faint himself. Amy's voice buzzed in his ear. "Anyway, I was calling for Shorty. One of the girls is giving him a manicure. He wanted me to tell you he won't be in at all today. He needs to do some shopping."

"Shorty? Shopping?"

"Jake, what's with you today? You're the one who told me about Shorty being color blind, so I offered to go shopping with him. Harvey's given him a list of colors and styles. I thought I'd let you know I won't have time to make dinner."

Jake took a deep breath. "That's fine. Have a nice time and I'll catch you later."

And he meant it. He would catch her. All his doubts had dissolved under the fear of having lost her to Shorty. He felt like a reprieved man. This was it. He'd made up his mind. If he had to marry her to curtail her wild schemes, then, by God, he'd marry her. She could forget her ideas about finding a "level-headed, liberated husband."

But how could he convince her to agree? Jake leaned back in his chair, considering. He doubted she'd believe him if he told her he'd had a sudden change of heart, that he wanted to get married. Besides, she didn't consider him a qualified candidate, anyway.

Part of the problem was she couldn't forget the brother-sister relationship they'd had in the past. Somehow he had to make her see him in a new light. Why not take her on a date?

Jake frowned, picking up a pencil and flipping it thoughtfully. But would she go? Amy could be pretty stubborn once she had an idea in her head, and she was determined to find husband prospects.

Maybe the best way to catch her was in her own trap.

Dropping the pencil, he straightened in his chair. Now *there* was an idea. He'd tell her they were going out to check out possible husbands. Once out with him, in a different setting, she was bound to see they'd moved beyond their old relationship.

Jake linked his hands behind his head. Yeah, that was the answer. Amy's husband-hunting days were numbered. He'd take her out tonight.

"This is it?" Amy asked as Jake shifted gears and the truck rolled to a stop. She stared across the darkened parking lot at the innocuous building with Bee-Bop flashing in neon lights overhead. Tucked in a corner of a shopping center, the dance club didn't look like much from the outside.

"Yeah." Jake turned, laying his arm along the back of the seat. He studied her delicate profile in the light filtering through the windshield. Reaching out, he gently touched a pearl stud nestled against her ear-lobe. "Still hurt?"

"Not anymore." Amy watched as he climbed out of the truck and walked around to her side. Sometimes, she thought with a little ache in her chest, Jake could be so sweet. He asked about her earrings, he'd listened as she'd told him about Shorty's "conversion." He'd even offered to escort her to this club so she could meet some eligible men.

Yeah, Jake was a really nice guy.

He opened her door. With his hand on her elbow, she climbed down from the high seat. Her dress hiked up in the process, and he watched, frowning, as she yanked it back down her thighs. "I told you that dress is too short."

And sometimes, Amy mentally added, he was a pain. "The dress is fine."

"I liked the gray one, with the little collar."

"Then you should have worn it," she answered as they walked across the asphalt to the entrance. "*I* felt like wearing red. I wear the gray one to school board meetings."

"This one's too tight."

"It's supposed to be tight." Amy smiled at the burly young man guarding the doorway, then murmured to Jake, "Quit it, or I'll start in on *your* outfit."

Surprised, he looked down at his jeans and white pullover shirt. "What's wrong with what I'm wearing?"

She pretended to stifle a yawn. "Not much. It's just a little boring."

"Boring!"

Feeling vindicated by his annoyed tone, she began to open her black clutch purse to pay her share of the cover charge. Jake's glare stopped her and she snapped the purse shut.

"Thanks, Jake," the young man said as he took the money. "Haven't seen you for a while. By the way, I like the lady's dress."

Amy smiled. Jake scowled. "Yeah, Franco. You and every other wanna-be stud in the place."

"Hey, you look okay, too," Franco added. "Conservative, but okay."

"I'm thrilled you think so," Amy heard Jake say dryly as she walked ahead of him into the building.

She paused in the doorway. Through the flickering light cast from rotating balls overhead, she could see a surprisingly small dance floor. The area was surrounded on all sides by long barlike tables with high stools from which vantage-point customers sat watching either the dancers or a large screen against one wall where a Beatles movie flickered silently.

The music was loud, fast and sixtyish. A disc jockey on a small stage next to the screen introduced each song with a barrage of wisecracks. Waitresses, dressed in cheerleader sweaters and saddle shoes, circled the room.

With a mixture of relief and disappointment, she noticed most of the customers were in pairs, with ages ranging from early twenties to an elderly couple—who looked eighty, at least—snuggled in a corner.

Jake moved up behind her and she said, "There doesn't seem to be too many people here."

"Yeah, the night's young." Feeling annoyed with her, Jake scanned the room. Damn, he hoped his plan didn't backfire. He hadn't expected her to wear such a sexy dress, especially since he'd mentioned—several times—that he liked the gray. Instead she wore one that clung to her slim curves in a way that was guaranteed to attract every male eye in the place.

Still, unless he took her home—and after managing to get her here, he didn't want to do that—there wasn't much he could do about it now. Except keep her out of sight as much as possible. With this objective in mind, he followed her, pleased that she appeared to be heading to a table in the rear.

Amy stopped suddenly, and he gently grabbed her waist to avoid bumping into her. "What are you doing?" he asked, looking down at her.

She frowned, meeting his eyes. "What am *I* doing? What are you doing following me? You know we can't sit together."

His jaw tightened. "What do you mean, we can't sit together?"

"If we sit together, everyone will assume we *are* together. You know, a couple."

He shrugged. "That's okay." He gave her a nudge to get her moving.

She stayed put. "Well, it isn't okay with me. If people think you're with me, nobody will approach me."

Yeah, exactly what he had in mind. He evaluated the determined expression on her face, deciding on the best tactic to get over this hurdle. He tried, "It's early yet. The place doesn't get cracking until after ten. Why don't we sit together for a while, and then I'll casually move off?"

Amy glanced at her watch. Only a little after eight. It sounded reasonable. She didn't want to sit around by herself for an hour, either. "All right."

He escorted her to the table in the rear, and Amy climbed up on the high stool he pulled out. Jake said something as he sat next to her, but, unable to hear him above the music, Amy made a helpless gesture. Immediately, he placed his arm around her shoulders, leaning closer. "Do you like it?"

"It's great." She tried to ignore the tingling awareness his arm was causing. "Thanks for taking the time to bring me. It was really sweet of you." She smiled up at him.

Jake smiled back, feeling like the big bad wolf confronting Little Red Riding Hood. He watched Amy's animated face for a minute, then asked, "See any prospects yet?"

Amy glanced around, inadvertently meeting the eyes of a bearded man seated across the room. She supposed Dr. Potocki would say he was a prospect, but he looked so...hairy. He winked at her, and she hastily averted her eyes. "Not yet."

Good, Jake thought. He tried to keep his satisfaction out of his voice as he said, "Don't worry. Something will come up."

"Yes."

A cheerleader sauntered over, and Jake asked Amy, "What would you like to drink?"

She pondered whether to stick her usual soft drink or have a mixed drink to help her relax. From the corner of her eye, she caught the bearded man staring again. She opted for a strawberry margarita.

Jake ordered a beer. "Have you been to many singles bars?" he asked Amy as the waitress moved off.

"A couple of times with friends, but never alone. Most recently, I went with a group from school." At the memory, she covered her eyes and shuddered. "It was terrible. The principal insisted on dancing almost every dance with me."

Jake's brows drew together. "The fat one? Did he make a pass at you?"

"Worse. He kept stepping on my feet."

Jake made a derisive noise and Amy added, "It hurt! I thought he'd broken my toes."

"So that's why they look like they do." Jake stood up. "I promise to stay off them. Come on and dance."

"No. I can't dance."

His hand captured hers. He pulled her to the dance floor. "You can dance."

Amy danced. By the time the third song had ended her stiff movements had loosened. She laughed and swayed in a way that made Jake's muscles tighten and his blood beat hotly through his veins. The music turned slow, and he hesitated, torn between the need to hold her in his arms and the need to get her out of sight of the men evaluating her face, her figure and, finally, the strength of the man with her. Caution won. Declaring he needed to cool off, he led her back to the table. Behind her back, he stared coldly at any man he caught ogling her as they passed.

"I thought you said you couldn't dance," he said as they sat back down.

"I never have like that before." Amy lifted the curls off the back of her neck to cool her perspiring nape. The movement caused her breasts to lift and thrust out against her dress. Jake took another drink, trying to concentrate on what she was saying. "I guess all the advice that students gave me when I chaperoned the Spring Fling paid off. Several of them insisted on showing me the 'in' steps. I didn't have the nerve to try them there, but you inspired me."

Amy picked up her sweet, fruity drink and took a sip. He did inspire her. Despite his muscular build, Jake had the fluid grace of a natural athlete. In the fitted white shirt he was wearing, he was, if not the most handsome, certainly the most masculine-looking man in the room, she thought. "Where did *you* learn to dance like you do?"

Jake answered, "Oh, I come here now and then."

Of course he did. Amy touched the moisture on her glass, watching a drop slide down the stem. He was single. He was healthy. He was a man. When Jake had lived with Maddie, an endless array of women had paraded through his life. Why would he have changed? Jake was the perpetual bachelor.

She finished her drink and set down her glass. Really, it was none of her business. She had her own life to worry about. She looked around the room. It was starting to get crowded. "Maybe you should sit somewhere else now. I think I'm going to try one of the book's techniques."

Jake didn't budge. Techniques? Someday, he decided, he'd burn that book. "What does the book advise?" he asked, hoping to distract her.

"To be discreetly aggressive." Amy leaned toward him confidingly. "Dr. Potocki recommends one trick that is very effective."

"Really? What is it?"

She looked around to make sure no one was listening. Jake obligingly lowered his head so she could speak in his ear. Her sweet breath blew softly against his cheek as she said, "What you do is make eye contact, and then break it." She sat back.

He looked at her. "That's all?"

"Yes."

"It sounds too simple."

"It is simple. But effective."

"I don't believe it."

"It's true. I'll show you."

Amy looked down at the table. Jake watched her, slightly amused. To think he'd been worried that she had an idea that might work.

Suddenly, she looked up. Her eyes were widened, looking directly into his with so much sensual invitation his breath caught. Desire sparked and flared into flame. Instinctively, he began leaning toward those inviting blue depths, but before he could move, she lowered her gaze again.

He froze, waiting for her to look back at him. She didn't. Instead she toyed with her drink, glanced around the room, watched the movie. Finally, unable to stand it any longer, he said, "Amy."

Immediately, her gaze flew back to his. However, the sensual creature he'd glimpsed so briefly had disappeared, hidden behind the laughter that now filled her eyes. "Well?" she demanded. "Did it work or not?"

A game. She'd been playing a game with him, and even forewarned, he'd fallen for it. He took a sip of beer, working to control the surge of anger the realization caused. "Not," he lied.

"Maybe you're immune," Amy said lightly. "Or perhaps that's one place the book is wrong."

He forced a smile. "Apparently." That damn book. Hopefully, she wouldn't be trying that gambit with anyone else. Frowning at the thought, he set down his beer mug and grabbed her hand. "Let's dance."

He led her out on the dance floor. Desire still simmering, he pulled her close and wrapped his arms tightly around her slender waist.

Amy's arms circled his muscular neck. The drink had helped her relax, she thought. She had a strange, floaty feeling every time Jake's thighs rubbed against hers.

Because it was so invitingly close, she rested her cheek against his hard chest. She liked this place. She liked old songs. She shut her eyes, surrendering to the heavy beat and the warmth of Jake's arms. In a little while, she told herself, she'd make an effort to remember her plan and forget how comfortable it felt being held by Jake. Songs didn't last long.

And this one seemed especially short. With an effort, she opened her eyes when it ended. Slowly, she removed her arms from his neck.

Even more slowly, Jake released her, too. The deejay had flipped on a fast record, and "Sunshine Superman" by Donovan burst into the room. Jake steered her off the floor and back to their seats as Donovan warned, "Babe, I'm gonna make you mine."

Jake picked up his beer, his gaze fastened on Amy. He wanted to dance close with her again, and he didn't think he could wait through another long set of fast songs. Muttering a short, "Excuse me," he left Amy to persuade the deejay to play a slow one.

Amy watched him weave through the dancers. Where was he going? He'd looked so determined—almost angry.

She tracked his progress across the room, critically eyeing his broad back and slim hips. Yes, even from this angle, he looked good. She picked up her glass, finishing off the ice melting in the bottom. Her limbs still felt heavy, rather like moving underwater. Even the music and conversations seemed muted. The only clear thing in the room was Jake. Funny, she had never noticed before just how handsome he actually was.

Apparently, she wasn't the only one who thought so. Amy's eyes narrowed as a slim red-haired woman walked up and threw her arms around his neck. He returned the hug, listened to what she said, and after accepting a final kiss on the cheek, turned back to talk to the disc jockey as the woman moved away.

Suddenly, Amy's pleasantly lethargic feeling disappeared, and the room came back into focus. She crossed her arms, hugging her chest. She felt tired. And lonely.

She forced herself to sit up straighter. What a fool she was! Obviously, Jake was doing what she'd asked. He was moving away, making it possible for other men to approach her. Why was she wasting time, mooning over him instead of looking for a man?

She glanced up, and again her eyes met those of the bearded man. He smiled. Tentatively, Amy smiled back.

Later that night, Jake sat in his darkened living room trying to figure out why his plan had backfired. They'd talked. They'd danced. He'd gone to request a slow number, said "hi" to an old friend, and when he'd returned, Amy was on the floor dancing with a bearded stranger.

Jake had cut in, and she hadn't protested, but something had changed. She'd retreated emotionally somehow, keeping him at an impersonal distance he hadn't been able to breach. They'd left soon after, and she hadn't talked much on the way home. Once there, she'd gone up to bed leaving him literally in the dark.

Damn! What had gone wrong?

She must have known he wanted her. His stomach dropped sickeningly as he carried the thought through to its conclusion. She hadn't wanted him.

Wearily, he ran his fingers through his hair. What *should* he do, what *could* he do, now? How did you make someone want you when they didn't? It was impossible.

Oh, Amy might believe you could make someone marry you by using tricks in a book, but he knew better. Jake sat up. Or did he?

He reached out and turned on the lamp. The book was on the coffee table. He picked it up and studied the cover. Did it work? Amy thought it did, and the eye contact she'd demonstrated on him certainly had. Possibly, so had the "heart beat" theory. Could the book be valid?

After all, Joan Potocki was a doctor. She must have some credibility. The back cover said she'd sold over a million copies. Was the answer to his problem right here under his nose? Thoughtfully, Jake turned the book over and opened to the first chapter.

There was only one way to find out: he'd try it. To win Amy, he'd try just about anything.

Chapter Nine

He put his new plan into action the next day while Amy went out shopping. Dusk had fallen before he heard her return. Using his apron to wipe the sweat beading his forehead, he glanced around the kitchen. He'd planned to have it all spotless before she came home, but creating an enticing meal was more difficult—and more messy—than he'd anticipated. Pots and pans littered the stove. Flour he'd spilled and hurriedly tried to clean up with a wet washcloth formed a gooey paste across the countertop. Still, as he looked at the table he felt a surge of satisfaction.

The scarred oak was covered by a white lace tablecloth Amy had unearthed from a chest upstairs but never used. He'd managed to find two dinner plates with the same blue pattern, and all the silverware matched. Two candles left over from last Halloween—one black and one orange—were stuck in empty beer bottles to serve as a centerpiece.

Hearing Amy's heels clicking toward the kitchen, he quickly lit the candles and turned out the light. Perfect.

"Jake? What's that smell? Did you burn something?" She opened the door and paused, staring at the table before her eyes swung around to meet his. She switched on the overhead light, her eyes widening as she looked beyond him at the stove and countertops.

Jake quickly strode across the room and switched off the light again. "No, I didn't *burn* anything. I made dinner." He grinned at her. She smiled warily back.

He wanted to kiss her wariness away. With the help of the book, he was going to marry her—she'd be his wife. The surge of elation the thought caused startled him. Hoping the candlelight hid his expression, he let his gaze slide over her. She looked good in the white blouse and short denim skirt she had on. White leather sandals completed the outfit. Her hair curled in wild ringlets around her small head and he resisted the urge to tousle it further, indulging himself instead with one more glance along her slender figure, and back up to her suspicious eyes.

He turned away to avoid her gaze. She wasn't ready to hear yet that he was the guy she was searching for. The last thing he wanted to do was put her on her guard. He'd lull her back into feeling at ease with him again, then gradually reel her in, bit by bit, with his new behavior and tactics. Anxious to begin, he nodded toward a chair.

She remained rooted in the doorway. She slanted a glance up at him. "What's going on? Why the candles?"

He said smoothly, "The candles add atmosphere. Things have been a little tense between us the past couple of days and I thought a good dinner would ease us back into our old friendly status." He carried the serving dish over to the table, nudging her with his elbow as he passed. "Come on. Think of this as a peace offering. I made fried octopus."

She focused on the platter in his hands. "Octopus? You actually made fried octopus?" she asked in disbelief.

"I had to find something unusual to impress such a great cook. I went out to the fish market, had a long talk with one of the fresh fish vendors on the pier, and *voilà!* Octopus à la Jake." With a flourish, he put down the dish and pulled out her chair.

Reluctantly, Amy sat down. The evening was not going as she'd anticipated. After last night, she'd wanted to talk seriously about how, from now on, she'd handle the husband hunt on her own. With Jake, things somehow seemed to go wrong. She also wanted to ease the slight tension that existed between them. Now it seemed she didn't need to. Obviously, he'd reached the same conclusions on his own. Tonight, he was only concerned with forcing a strange fish—or was octopus a reptile?—down her throat.

He put some on her plate and she poked at one of the rubbery morsels with her fork. "Looks great, but—" she pasted on an expression of deep regret "—unfortunately, I'm allergic to octopus."

He wasn't impressed with her acting. "No, you're not. I'm positive you've never tried it in your life."

He was right, and as far as Amy was concerned, she could spend the rest of her life without it. Still, it *was* a peace offering. Besides, Jake in the candlelight, wearing one of her pink gingham aprons and with a smear of flour on his lean, tanned cheek, was hard to resist.

He speared a piece of octopus on his fork and held it up to her lips. She pressed them firmly closed. "Come on, Amy," he coaxed. "It took me over three hours to make this. I did it just for you."

"You shouldn't have," she mumbled, and he cunningly inserted the food into her slightly open mouth. Unable to resist his pleading look, she parted her lips further and he nudged the morsel in.

It sat on her tongue tasting like... octopus. Rubbery, yucky octopus. She considered swallowing it whole, but reluctantly abandoned the idea. Somehow, choking on octopus sounded like such an undignified way to die.

Slowly, she bit down. As she'd suspected, it was rubbery all the way through. She felt like she was gnawing on a piece of tire. Jake was watching expectantly, though, so she continued chewing. And chewing. By the time a minute had passed her jaws ached and the octopus was as unpalatable as ever.

In desperation, she pretended to swallow, and sent him a beaming smile. She pushed away from the table, mumbling, "Excuse me. I have to use the bathroom."

Jake watched her disappear and looked at the remaining cephalopod in resignation. When Barney, the old sea-worn vendor, had told him octopus was an aphrodisiac, he'd had his doubts. "Octopus?" he'd echoed.

The wrinkled face beneath the mariner's cap nodded. "Sure thing, sonny. Them Romans and Greeks used to gobble 'em up. Almost as good as a love potion is octopuses.''

"Octopi.''

"Octo pie?'' The vendor scratched his shaggy, white head. "Never made that. I usually pound and fry it.'' He'd puffed out his bony chest. "Works for me.''

Well, Jake had had his doubts about the fish story. Which was why he'd prepared another item on the menu that was a surefire winner.

When Amy returned a few minutes later, he was reaching into the oven. As she sat down at the table again, he said, "I can see you're resisting the octopus, so here's something less exotic for you to munch on.'' He placed a crusty brown loaf in front of her.

"Jake, it looks delicious.'' Amy was impressed. Baking a loaf of bread took time and effort. She sniffed the rich, yeasty smell appreciatively. "Mmm. What kind is it?''

"Beer.''

"I beg your pardon?'' She raised her eyebrows questioningly. "I thought you said beer.''

"I did.'' Tilting back his chair, he reached into a drawer and produced a knife. "Surely an expert homemaker such as yourself has heard of making bread with beer?''

"Yes, but I've never tasted it.'' She watched with interest as he began slicing the loaf.

Or perhaps hacking was a better word, she thought. It almost looked like he was sawing wood. He finally managed to break through the hardened crust only to discover the inside was moist and doughy.

Deflated, he looked down at the mess. "Maybe it tastes better than it looks. Would you like to try it?''

His expression was hopeful but she shook her head. "I've had my fill of experiments for one evening. You go ahead."

"I'll pass." Jake set down the knife. "That's all I had time to make. Are you still hungry?"

Amy ignored her growling stomach. She didn't think she could face another of Jake's concoctions tonight. "Not at all. Maybe we can make some popcorn later." Pushing back her chair, she began piling dishes.

Jake caught her hands to stop her. "I said I'd clean up and I will." She started to argue. On an inspiration, he added, "At the end of a long day, it kind of soothes me to put my hands in warm water."

Amy looked surprised. "You never told me that."

"Yeah, well, I didn't want to be greedy and hog all the fun."

"That's so sweet, Jake." She smiled, patting his shoulder. "Well, from now on you do them all you want. I hate washing dishes."

She went into the living room. Jake savored the memory of how warmly her blue eyes had shone. Squaring his shoulders, he blew out the flickering candles and began clearing the table. Being a liberated man was—as he'd always suspected—not a lot of fun. Still, Amy's smile was some compensation. Plunging his arms into the soapy water, he grimaced. He hated to do dishes, too.

He scrubbed at a tenacious piece of octopus clinging to a platter while planning his next strategy. His first plan, winning Amy's attention through her stomach, hadn't worked—yet, at any rate. He'd have to keep cooking. When he finished cleaning up tonight, he'd try plan two: what Amy's Dr. Potocki called "mirroring."

He'd found the section very interesting. According to Dr. Potocki, mirroring a person's physical posture was one of the easiest, most powerful getting-close techniques that anyone could use. By matching a person's movements, expressions, even clothing, if possible, the person being copied, or the "copee," felt an unconscious sense of approval toward the "copier."

An hour later he walked into the living room prepared to start. Amy had showered. Her curls were damp, and she'd changed into shorts and a sleeveless blue shirt. She was watching a silly sitcom with her bare feet propped on the coffee table.

Great. No problem here. Plopping down next to her, he put his feet on the table alongside hers.

Leaning back, he tried to watch the program. His gaze slowly wandered to Amy's legs. How sexy they looked. Tan. Slender. So smooth, he wanted to run his hands up to...

Uh, oh. Resolutely he forced his attention back to the television. She wasn't ready for anything like that, even though he was. He shifted uncomfortably. Almost too ready.

To his relief, she distracted him from his thoughts by crossing her ankles. Now things were getting going. He waited a few seconds and crossed his also. She ran a hand through her hair, and he did the same then let his hands fall as limply to his sides as hers were.

Amy yawned, reminding him of a sleepy kitten. He yawned, too, watching her from beneath half-closed lids. She looked so cuddly, so kissable, with her face scrubbed clean of makeup and her hair curling wildly. He liked the pearl studs on the pink lobes of her ears.

Someday, he'd kiss her there, and run his tongue along the small shell of her ear. He'd kiss along her delicate jaw, and up over her pink cheeks. He'd taste her all over.

He stifled a groan. Please, God, let his plans work fast. Waiting for her to choose him was becoming harder by the minute.

She was moving again. He tensed slightly, prepared to "mirror" her. Casually, she reached over and picked up a small bottle of nail polish off the table. He watched in horrified fascination as she drew her knees beneath her chin, and bent over to carefully apply the polish to her toenails.

No way he could get in that position. If his back didn't give out, his knees would surely do so.

Impatiently, he waited for her to finish. Mirroring her posture wasn't the only technique the book recommended, he reminded himself. Another primal way to get close to your beloved was to breathe in the same pattern as he or she did.

He'd try that. He watched her as she slowly drew the tiny black brush over each pink nail, finally finishing and recapping the bottle. She settled back again, stretching out her legs and wiggling her toes, chuckling at the action on TV.

Jake moved a little closer to her. He frowned a little. Funny, but he'd never noticed before that Amy breathed so rapidly. He shrugged. Oh, well. He began breathing in synchronization with her.

One breath, pause. Two breaths, pause. He inhaled the unpleasant smell of her polish. Three breaths, pause. By the time he reached ten, he felt nauseous but determinedly kept going...

Amy sat perfectly still, pretending to watch the program. She couldn't say exactly how or why, but Jake was acting *strange.* Octopus? Strange. He enjoyed doing dishes? Very strange. Now he was so quiet. The fine hairs on her nape prickled; he was watching her. She was sure of it. She darted a glance at him, but he was staring at the television. Very, very strange indeed.

And why had he moved closer? Tension radiated from him, and a corresponding reaction began building in her breasts and abdomen. She hoped he wasn't thinking about making love to her. Her nipples tightened at the thought. Okay, she was hoping, but she *shouldn't* be. Darn it, what would she do if he tried? He wouldn't. He was happy to be friends again and so was she. Logic, not lust, was the way to find a lasting relationship.

Her thoughts were interrupted by a gasping noise. She frowned, unable to pinpoint the source. Suddenly she realized it was Jake, breathing oddly. As she looked over, he swayed slightly. "Oh, my goodness! Jake, I think you're hyperventilating. What's wrong?"

She jumped up and shoved his face down to his knees. Why was she always rescuing this man?

Jake's blurring vision began to clear. Opening his eyes, he glared down at Amy's pink toenails, unconsciously echoing her thoughts. Why was he always choking or fainting around this woman?

No doubt about it. Amy was a pain.

Irritably, he resisted her restraining hand on the back of his neck. "For God's sake, I'm fine, Amy! Let me up. I just got dizzy for a minute. It could happen to anyone."

Pushing her hand away, he stood up. He felt like an absolute, complete fool. He also felt sick from the smell of the polish. Staggering a little, he headed for his bed. He'd have to call it quits tonight, but next time would be another story.

He'd overwhelm her.

"Jake, I'm overwhelmed." Beaming, Amy accepted the small, rectangular box wrapped in silver foil that Jake offered as he came in the door two evenings later.

She didn't know what had come over him lately. He'd made dinner every night, did dishes alone and hardly let her lift a finger with the housework.

Most of the changes in Jake made her uneasy, wondering if he was tired of having her around the house. This change, however, was a pleasant surprise. Receiving gifts for no apparent occasion was a habit she'd encourage.

She shook the oblong box experimentally. It felt a little heavy. Chocolates! she decided happily. The dear sweet man had given her a one-pound box of chocolates. What a wonderful guy! No one had ever given her chocolates before.

Feeling strangely shy, she smiled at him. Jake grinned broadly back. In a white T-shirt and worn jeans, with his hair endearingly mussed, he leaned in the doorway, watching her. Feeling self-conscious with his gray eyes studying her, she carefully pulled off the paper, then stared at the box in her hands.

It wasn't chocolates.

On the cover, a leotard-clad woman posed with her firm bosom thrust forward and her hands on perfectly proportioned hips. That scum, that lowlife, that no-good, rotten Jake, had given her an exercise tape.

He leaned forward eagerly. "How do you like it?" The next second he ducked as Amy threw the box at him and went storming past to her room.

"Amy, wait! What's the matter?"

Pausing with her foot on the first step, Amy turned with a fierce expression. "You know what the matter is!"

Bewildered, he stared at her and spread out his hands. "No, I don't."

She glared at him. "You gave me an exercise tape, Jake. Logically it follows that you think I'm fat. Well, you can just forget about those chocolate almond cookies you're so fond of, buster! You won't be seeing those, or any other dessert, for quite a while."

Surprise, comprehension and remorse passed swiftly across Jake's face. Lamely, he said. "Ah, Amy. I'm sorry. Of course I don't think you're fat."

"Oh? Then why did you give me that tape?"

Jake stood staring blankly at her. He couldn't admit he'd given it to her to increase her heartbeat so she'd find him more attractive, like the book suggested. Desperately, he tried to think of another answer.

When he didn't reply, Amy's small chin lifted in the air. Turning, she headed up into her room, making a point of slamming the door loudly behind her.

"Amy! Darling, how are you?"

"Maddie." Gripping the receiver, Amy swallowed to ease the unexpected constriction in her throat. Until she heard the other woman's voice, she hadn't realized how much she'd missed her. Maddie sounded so happy, so loving, so *normal*. "Where are you? Are you having fun?"

"We stopped at this sweet little island, and darling, I can't begin to tell you what a wonderful time I'm having! Not that I mean to try, the reason I'm calling is to find out how you and that grandson of mine are."

"I'm fine, Maddie." Amy hesitated. "Jake's fine too."

"Oh? You don't sound very sure of that. Is something wrong?"

"No. Well, I don't think so." Amy sighed, relieved to have someone she trusted to discuss her worries with. "It's just he's been acting a little...strange."

"Strange? What do you mean?"

Amy peeked around the kitchen door. The living room was empty; Jake had left. She stretched the phone cord over to a kitchen chair and sat down. "I mean different. Weird. Maddie, he insists on making dinner every night."

"How sweet!"

"Well, yes. But the dinners he makes are terrible. Last night the highlight of the meal was oyster pudding."

There was silence at the other end of the line for a moment. "Oh, dear."

"Yes," Amy said, pleased Maddie understood. "That's not all. He cleans."

The older woman laughed. "Darling, I know Jake has never been overly neat, still—"

"You don't understand." Holding the receiver closer, Amy lowered her voice for emphasis. "He was late to work today because he wanted to *sweep under the beds*."

"No!" Maddie sounded fascinated. "What else?"

Amy frowned, trying to explain. "Well, he breathes. Not that that's strange, of course. It's just the way he does it. Loudly and in erratic spurts. And, oh, yes! He's becoming an exercise fanatic."

"He's always run every day—"

"Not for himself. For me. He's so concerned about it, I finally agreed to jog over to his latest job this afternoon just so he'd quit bothering me."

"Hmm." Maddie paused. "This is rather odd, dear, but cooking, cleaning, breathing and exercising doesn't exactly sound *dangerous*."

"I guess not." Standing up, Amy began pacing. She rubbed her temple where a headache was forming. Jake's behavior was dangerous. She, for one, was in danger of losing her sanity.

"Enough about my aggravating grandson," Maddie said briskly. "How is your exciting plan going?"

Amy sighed. "Not so well, Maddie. Jake introduced me to a couple of guys, but they weren't right. We also tried a singles bar. I'm beginning to wonder if the whole thing can even work."

Maddie gave a throaty chuckle. "Take it from me, darling. It does."

Amy froze in the middle of the kitchen. "Do you mean . . . ?"

"*Yes!* There aren't too many single, older men on this trip, but darling, I have *two* practically fighting for my attention."

"Oh, my goodness." Amy groped for a chair and plopped down. "How did you do it?"

"I followed the book! Dr. Potocki is *wonderful*. I speak in quieter, lower tones. I walk with optimum posture for meeting men, and I don't neglect a single opportunity. At my age, I can't afford to. In other words, when a man shows interest, I go out with him. How else can I discover if he's Mr. Right?"

"And have you found Mr. Right?"

"Well, no. But I'm having a lot of fun trying. So, darling, what's holding you up?"

What *was* holding her up? Amy frowned. "I'm not sure, Maddie. I guess I've been so busy worrying about Jake, I haven't thought much about it. I haven't even told him yet that I'll be trying on my own."

"I see. That's very interesting, darling." Maddie was quiet a moment. Suddenly she chuckled. "Tell him today, dear."

Amy's head throbbed a little. She pressed her fingers against the pain. "I'm not sure—"

"I am. Tell him, darling. Or better yet, show him. *Promise* me the first chance you get to go out with someone, you'll do it. After all, if you don't try, you'll never know if your plan will work, dear. Don't let Jake get in the way of your dreams."

Amy sighed. Maddie was right. Someday she'd regret not trying harder to find her perfect match. She didn't want to live her life alone, or with someone she wasn't compatible with. She wanted a home and a family. Her trouble was she'd let her confusion over Jake's behavior distract her from her goal. Well, not anymore. "I promise, Maddie."

"Wonderful, darling! I'll see you in a couple of weeks and we can compare notes. Give my love to Jake."

"I will. Take care." Amy set down the receiver. She jumped, startled when it immediately rang again. She snatched it up. "Maddie?"

"I've been called a lot of names in my time, but never Maddie," an attractive baritone voice answered. "Is this Jake Weston's number?"

"Yes, it is. May I take a message?" Amy pulled open Jake's "junk" drawer and began scrambling through it for a pencil. She found one, regarded its broken lead in disgust and threw it down as the caller spoke again.

"Sure. I'm Howie—Howie Anderson. I'm calling to tell Jake I'll be a little late this afternoon. I've been away for a few months and want to check on how the house he's building is going. Has he left?"

"Yes, about half an hour ago. I can give him your message, though. I'll be meeting him in a little while myself."

"Thanks." There was a short pause, then Howie added, "Jake told me a friend of his grandmother's—is it Amy?—would be staying with him for a while."

"I'm Amy."

His voice deepened in amusement. "Somehow, you don't sound a day over sixty."

She grinned. "Thank you. That's nice to hear since I'm only twenty-four."

"Twenty-four, huh? Somehow my old buddy neglected to mention that fact. Do you two have something going?"

Amy's smile faded. "Yes. Mutual respect and love for his grandmother."

"Oh. Sorry if I was out of line." Howie's voice deepened, and he added coaxingly, "Maybe we could go out to dinner, give me a chance to redeem myself."

About to refuse, Amy paused. Why not? Maddie was right. If she didn't go out, she'd never find Mr.

Right. Howie sounded nice, and he was a friend of Jake's. Remembering her promise to his grandmother, she said cautiously, "Maybe we could."

"That's great. If you're going to be at Jake's job site, watch for me. If I miss you, I'll call back later."

"Okay. See you then." Hanging up the phone, Amy took a deep breath. She'd done it. She'd taken a logical step forward on her plan. Maddie would be proud of her.

Jake would probably be happy, too. He'd probably been doing all the cooking and cleaning so she'd have more time to find a husband. Or maybe it was his way of telling her she wasn't needed around here anymore.

The thought caused a little ache in her chest. Well, if that was the reason, he'd be glad to hear about Howie. She'd tell him this afternoon.

Chapter Ten

J ake stood on the sloping roof of the Cape Cod-style home. The house, with its gleaming bay windows and blue-gray trim, was finally finished. He savored a surge of satisfaction. His crew, as usual, had done a fine job.

Every house he built caused the same sense of pride to well up in his chest. As a contractor, he felt the way a conductor of an orchestra must feel creating beautiful music. Only his music was homes, quality homes, where people would laugh, play and live together. People like Amy and him.

He looked toward the sidewalk running along the bay. It was filled with people: some jogging, some strolling, others whizzing along on their in-line skates. There wasn't a sign of her yet, but it shouldn't be long now.

This was his last attempt using Dr. P.'s methods. None of the book's methods appeared to be making a dent in the protective, friendly reserve Amy displayed whenever she was around him. If this didn't work, he'd burn the book and follow his own instincts to catch Amy, the instincts clamoring for him to make love to her until she agreed that he was the right man for her.

Squinting into the bright afternoon sun, he checked to see what his crew was doing. Shorty was out of sight, probably tiling the master bathroom. Rod was doing some finishing work in the garage, and Harris had left to pick up more cement.

Everyone was busy. Jake breathed a sigh of relief. Now, if they'd only stay that way. He was worried enough about his plan without wondering what the guys might think of his erratic behavior.

He wished he could have raised her heartbeat at some other place, but he didn't want to waste any more time and he'd already arranged to meet Howie here. He couldn't put Howie off because Howie'd designed this house and was anxious to view the completed project. His old college buddy had become a prominent architect, and whenever possible, they sent work each other's way. It was an arrangement that benefited both of them.

He hoped Amy turned up before Howie did. It had taken some fast talking to persuade her to go jogging at all after the disaster with the exercise tape, but she'd finally agreed.

Now, the bait was set. Basically, the success of his plan to make Amy want him depended on two factors. First, increasing her heartbeat up to the recommended rate, which would happen when she jogged over, and secondly, her unawareness of what he was doing as he posed for her edification. If she realized what was going on, it might not work.

Jake decided his muscles could best be displayed if he was doing something active. That way, when he flexed, it wouldn't look too obvious. With this in mind, he picked up a shingle and nail bag that he'd carried up for that purpose.

Suddenly, he spotted Amy in the distance, jogging along on the sidewalk. She wasn't going too fast, he noticed. She slowed to a walk for a moment, and Jake grinned. Amy really did hate anything that caused her to sweat.

Still, she was moving faster than he'd expected. Her heartbeat should be just about right. He checked for his men again and then peeled off his white T-shirt. The sun and breeze felt good on his bare shoulders, but Jake grimaced. He must have worked without his shirt a thousand times before, yet somehow he felt foolish undressing and parading around with the express purpose of impressing Amy.

But a man had to do what a man had to do. He paused a moment, watching her figure come closer, her bright pink shirt and dark shorts specks of color against a backdrop of white sand. The book said that men are more attracted to a good-looking woman when their hearts are beating faster, and he saw no reason the hypothesis shouldn't work equally well in reverse. He just hoped Amy viewed him as at least passably attractive.

She was close enough now so he could see more clearly what she was wearing. Jake frowned. In his opinion, her pink sleeveless shirt was much too tight against her gently bouncing breasts. The frown deepened to a scowl. Her shorts were certainly no better. If the damn things were any smaller, she might as well forget about them altogether.

Amy must have caught sight of him at that moment because she lifted a hand in greeting. Jake quickly averted his gaze to make it appear he hadn't seen her yet.

From the corner of his eye, he watched her nearing the job site. Swaggering to the edge of the roof, he flexed his right bicep, holding the shingle up. His silhouette had to be clear from this position.

In case it wasn't, he made his way over to another peak. This time he bent down and hammered an invisible nail into the roof. He quickly glanced down the length of his body. Would it look good to her? His tan was so dark—too dark? She'd never mentioned what she thought of the color of his eyes, or his hair, for that matter. His body had always been a capable tool he kept in good shape. Wondering if Amy liked it or not was making him feel uneasy. He'd have to just continue on the assumption that she did.

He glanced down to the sandy lot below. Amy was standing at the front of the house, shading her eyes with her hand as she looked up at him. The pose lifted her pink shirt, exposing her golden brown, flat stomach. Jake frowned again.

Amy lifted her hand to wave but let it drop, her smile fading when she saw Jake's expression. Since the night they'd gone dancing, he'd been acting strange, but at least he'd been friendly. Today, however, he looked almost fierce.

"Hi, Jake. I made it," she called up.

"Yeah. Hi."

Amy waited, but he didn't add anything more. He must have some kind of back pain, she decided, watching the way he was contorting and stretching. Finally, she asked, "Are you almost done?"

"Yeah. Give me a minute to finish up here."

Jake strutted to another area and crouched down, making sure, however, that he was still in Amy's view. He was working on another invisible nail when he became aware of Shorty calling him from the back of the house.

"Hey, boss!"

Dammit. Couldn't he up Amy's heartbeat in peace? Irritated, Jake stalked to the back of the roof and looked down at the top of Shorty's red hair.

"What?"

Shorty stared up, his round face creased in puzzlement. "What're you doing?"

Jake put his hands on his hips and glared down. "What does it look like I'm doing?"

"I dunno."

"I'm working on the roof."

"Oh."

The question answered, Jake waited for Shorty to head back into the house. Shorty didn't move.

"Uh, boss . . ."

"What?"

"We finished the roof four days ago. Don't you remember?"

"Yes, I remember. I'm just hitting down a few more nails."

Shorty looked surprised. "You mean Harris left nails hanging out?"

"Yes. No. Dammit, is that bathroom finished?"

"Sure is." Shorty beamed up at him.

Damn. "Well, why don't you head on home," Jake said finally.

Shorty's eyebrows shot up toward his receding hairline. "Head home? At two o'clock on a Wednesday?"

"That's right."

Shorty's surprised expression changed to one of pleasure. "Thanks, boss. I think Sue is home today. Maybe we can catch a baseball game or something."

"Great."

No sooner had Shorty left than Rod wandered up, apparently done with the garage. "Whatcha doing up there, Jake?"

Jake sighed. "Just a minute." He stomped to the other side of the house and looked down. Amy was no longer standing in the unplanted yard. She'd moved over to a spreading magnolia tree nearby, taking advantage of the shade provided. Someone, possibly Shorty, had left a lounger there, and she was sprawled out on it.

She wasn't even looking at him. He wasn't sure, but from this angle, it even looked like she had her eyes closed.

"Amy. Hey, Amy!" He was right. She *did* have them closed. Hearing his voice jerked her up into a sitting position. "Are you going to sleep down there or something?"

Amy stifled a yawn. She'd thought she'd come for the exercise. Well, she'd exercised and now she was tired. Sleepless nights thinking about Jake were catching up with her.

She looked up at him, standing with his arms akimbo on the roof. His hair was tousled by the breeze, and one errant curl hung down over his eyes. His bare chest gleamed with a faint sheen of sweat in the hot sunlight. The muscles in his arms bulged. His tool belt rode low on his hips, reminding her of a gunfighter's holster. A hot wave of desire burned up from Amy's stomach to her breasts. The flush dissipated as she looked higher at his angry eyes, lowered brows and the tight line of his mouth.

What on earth was wrong now? He was acting strange all right, and she'd just about had enough of it. She'd forgiven him for giving her that insulting tape, and that had taken a lot of forgiving. She'd jogged over here in the noonday sun without a word of complaint. Nor had she complained about the husband prospects that Jake had picked out.

Now that she thought about it, *she* was the one who should be angry. Thanks to Jake, she hadn't made much headway finding Mr. Right, and the end of her vacation was only a couple of weeks off. Her lips firmed. Maddie was right; she wouldn't give up. No longer was that grumpy male on the roof going to interfere in *her* life.

Jake wasn't too happy with the expression on Amy's face. She didn't look like she was pulsating with awakened sexual desire. In fact, she didn't look like she liked him even one little bit.

He was searching for a way to change her expression back into the welcoming one she'd worn as she arrived, when Rod shouted again from the other side of the building. "Hey, Jake!"

Jake sighed. "Stay there," he ordered Amy. "I'll be right back."

"How thrilling," Amy muttered, glaring up at him.

She was definitely looking at him now, Jake noticed. This was his chance. Satisfied that her attention—at least for the moment—was fully focused on him, he lifted his arms, bending his elbows and curling his fists in a classic weightlifter's stance. He took a quick peek at his biceps. Hard as a rock. Had to be at least twenty inches around. Not bad for a guy who was pushing thirty-one and—in Amy's opinion—past his prime.

Yeah, not bad at all if he did say so himself. And it looked as if he had to say it himself: Amy sure didn't look impressed.

He gave her a final view of his chest, anyway, before turning away toward the back of the house where Rod waited, patiently looking up.

"So, what's up?" Rod asked.

Jake sighed. Here we go again. "I'm knocking in some loose nails."

Rod's eyes widened. "Harris left some loose—"

"No, I'm just checking to make sure he didn't," Jake interrupted.

"Need any help?"

"What I need," Jake said through gritted teeth, "is to be left alone. Why don't you take the rest of the day off?"

"But, Jake—"

"I know, I know. It's only two o'clock on Wednesday. Do you want the afternoon off or not?"

Rod did. He left without another word.

Jake moved back up to the top of the peak. He lifted his hammer and gave an innocent shingle a couple of whacks. He caught a movement with his peripheral vision and glanced down to where he'd last seen Amy. She was still there, her hair glinting in the bright sunlight. Unfortunately, she was no longer alone. Howie was there, standing close to her. Too close, in Jake's opinion.

The hammer came down and Jake yelped as it hit his thumb. He stared at the throbbing digit in equal pain and surprise. How did Amy do this to him?

He shook the pain out, watching the two below laugh together like old friends. He couldn't hear what they were saying but he could see Amy was having no trouble at all relating to Howie.

Howie was dressed for success in a tailored gray suit. And there she stood in that flattering shirt and those short shorts, smiling up at the tall blond man as if she'd finally discovered . . . the man of her dreams.

Jake's scowl darkened. Don't get carried away, he told himself. They're just having a friendly discussion. She probably doesn't even notice that Howie is a good-looking son of a gun. After all, he'd never noticed it before, and he'd known the architect for years.

And she couldn't know yet that Howie had a good sense of humor—although she *was* laughing an awful lot. Nor would she realize that Howie loved kids, or even that he was touching her hair.

Jake stiffened. Touching her hair! By God, Howie was on stage three minutes after meeting Amy. *He'd* known Amy for ten years before they'd reached stage three.

Jake had never made it down the ladder as fast as he did in the following few minutes. Fast as he was, Howie was faster. As Jake approached the pair, he heard his ex-buddy Howie making arrangements to pick Amy up the following Saturday.

"I'm looking forward to it, Amy," Howie said, releasing her hand as Jake stalked up. "Hiya, Jake. How's it going, old buddy? I see you've been keeping busy." Howie's gaze was fixed on the newly completed house as he spoke.

Jake's gaze was fixed on Amy. "I notice you've been pretty busy yourself," he drawled. "I guess you and Amy have become acquainted."

Howie turned back to Amy and sent her a wide, white smile. Good teeth, too, Jake noted absently. "Amy and I met over the phone." He winked at her. "I'm going to take this old friend of Maddie's to the beach on Saturday."

Amy smiled at Howie, and Jake's gaze hardened. How dare she come running over here and let a man she'd never even met ask her out on a date? Or wear that shirt and those shorts in public? Or let Howie touch her hair—her *hair*, for heaven's sake—when she belonged to him!

Amy felt surprised when Jake looked at her with anger burning in his eyes. She'd expected him to be a little annoyed when he discovered she no longer needed his help finding a man; she hadn't expected him to be furious. At least Howie wasn't a stranger. He was a friend of Jake's. Her chin lifted. She refused to feel guilty. She'd told Jake from the start what she planned to do. He was just being overprotective.

They were locked in a stare-off when John Harris walked up. "Hey, Jake," the older man said as he joined the group. "What's this I hear about trouble with the roofing?"

Chapter Eleven

"No trouble, John," Jake answered without removing his gaze from Amy. "At least not with the roofing."

He slowly removed his tool belt. Amy's gaze slipped down over his chest as he pulled the buckle loose, and then back up to meet his eyes. A slight pink darkened her cheeks.

Jake watched as the delicate line of her jaw firmed. His own jaw tightened in response. They needed to get things settled, and he preferred to do it without an audience. Especially an audience that included one of her damn husband prospects.

He looked over at Howie, whose bland expression was belied by the laughter dancing in his blue eyes. "Do you mind if John shows you around?"

"Not at all," Howie answered promptly. "But I was hoping Amy would join us."

Without giving her a chance to respond, Jake said firmly, "Right now, Amy and I have a few things to discuss."

He turned to Harris and told his foreman, "I'm quitting for the day. As far as I'm concerned, you're welcome to do the same as soon as you've shown my *friend* here around and locked up."

Harris began to speak, and Jake wearily lifted his hand to forestall the remarks he could see coming. "Yes, I know it's only two o'clock on a Wednesday and that I never quit this early. Now, I'm leaving, damn it, and if you have any sense, you'll tie things up and do the same. Come on, Amy." He grabbed her arm and began hustling her toward the pickup truck.

Amy tried to dig in her heels but couldn't get traction on the sandy soil. "Jake, wait! I didn't say goodbye to—"

"The lady says goodbye, Harris," Jake called over his shoulder without looking back.

Amy added, "But what about—"

"Goodbye to you, too, Howie. I'll talk to you later," Jake yelled, not breaking his stride.

"Bye, Jake," Howie called back, his voice filled with amusement. "And goodbye, Amy. See you Saturday."

"See you then, Howie." Ignoring Jake's tight-lipped expression, she managed to wave to the two men still standing there watching, before Jake gently crammed her into the truck and slammed the door.

The trip back to the beach house was accomplished in silence and at a speed that exceeded the limit. Once home, Amy marched over to the couch and sat with her arms folded while Jake paced restlessly back and forth in front of her.

He hadn't bothered to put his shirt back on, she noticed. Somehow he looked more uncivilized, more savage, wearing blue jeans with his brown chest bare. Not that she was intimidated, she decided, tilting her chin.

Every so often, he'd stop, stare at her a moment, and then resume pacing, his boots clumping on the hardwood floor. Little clumps of mud had fallen off those boots and were slowly being ground into the polished wood. Amy bit her tongue. He might be making a mess, but after all, he'd been the one polishing the floors lately. It really wasn't her place to say anything. If she wanted him to stay out of her life, then she'd have to stay out of his.

Jake stopped in front of her again and glared down. Amy glared back. She hadn't seen him this angry since . . . well, she'd never seen him this angry.

"Are you really planning on going out with Howie on Saturday?"

She looked down and studied the polish on one of her nails. "Why shouldn't I?"

Jake said angrily, "Because I thought I was going to set you up on dates."

Amy's eyes narrowed. "So why didn't you set me up with Howie?"

"Because Howie's not right," he shot back. "I found you a couple of possibilities, didn't I?"

Amy raised her eyebrows. Shorty and Richard—possibilities? "Which one were you expecting me to choose, Jake?"

He folded his arms defensively as his eyes met hers. "They're both nice guys."

"Exactly." Amy sat up straighter on the sinking cushion. "They are both nice men. That's why Richard made an effort to entertain me even though he was scared to death of roller coasters. As for Shorty, he took me out from pity after you filled him up with a sad story about my lonely evenings. He's so in love with his Sue, the poor man could hardly see straight.''

Jake shrugged. ''They fit your specifications,'' he reminded her.

Amy threw up her hands. ''Yes, I know they fit my specifications, but where I made my big mistake was in getting you involved.''

''What do you mean by that?''

''I mean that neither Shorty nor Richard would ever have approached me on their own. Howie is the first one to be genuinely interested in me without any prodding.''

Jake snorted. ''Howie is interested in any woman under the age of forty.''

Amy bounced to her feet, shoulders stiff, fists clenched at her sides. ''Thank you very much! Just because you don't think I'm attractive, doesn't mean other men don't!''

Jake ran his hand through his hair in frustration. ''I didn't say you're not attractive. I think you're very attractive.''

''Hah!''

''I do!''

''Since when?'' she demanded.

''Since the day you tried the Heimlich maneuver on me weeks ago.''

Her eyes widened. Like a lawyer with an opposing witness, she pounced. ''The day you came in from jogging.''

''Yeah.''

''The day you were hot and sweaty.''

"I admit to being . . . hot," he drawled.

Ignoring his innuendo, she added, "The day your heart was beating faster and you saw a passably attractive woman. Namely me."

Despite himself, Jake's lips twitched at her accusing tone. "Yes, you."

"Aha!" Amy sat down on the couch with the air of someone who felt they had won their case.

Her tone was so knowing, so smug, that Jake gritted his teeth. "What do you mean, aha?"

"I mean, aha, that's why you don't want me to go out with Howie."

"What are you talking about?"

"What you feel is attraction 'caused by proximity and the right circumstances.' The book explains all about it. In other words, I'm convenient for you to desire right now," she explained simply.

Jake spoke through clenched teeth. "No, you're not. There's nothing convenient about you. In fact, most of the time—like right now—I think you're a first-class pain! I don't want you to go out with Howie because you belong with me."

Amy raised her eyebrows. "Your possessive feelings are a carryover from your desire to protect me when I was a child," she explained kindly.

Jake glared at her. "I didn't want to protect you when you were a child. I wanted to wring your neck. And if you don't stop playing amateur psychologist, I just might do it."

"Well, I'm not looking for a man who wants to wring my neck. I'm looking for someone nonthreatening and nonviolent, a liberated man who doesn't try to boss me around."

"I *am* nonthreatening and nonviolent, and I don't boss you around. I just don't want you to go out with Howie!" Jake shouted.

Her voice determined, she said, "Well, I am. Maddie would think it's a good idea and so do I. There's nothing wrong with it."

He stood up, towering over her. "What's wrong is that you don't want Howie. You want me. There are some things you can't hide from, Amy, and this is one of them."

Chapter Twelve

"Howie, did Jake force you to come to his beach party today?"

"Not exactly. Let's just say he can be very persuasive."

Persuasive? Trudging along beside the tall, blond man, Amy tried to catch his eye. Not easy since they were both loaded like mules with beach chairs, a blanket, a beach umbrella and stumbling through the sand under the hot afternoon sun.

Not that she expected him to elaborate or even give her a straight answer. Men had a strange code of honor. Howie had no problem going out with her, even though he knew Jake wasn't happy about the situation. At the same time, he refused to betray the methods Jake had used to turn their twosome at the beach into a party. Howie was obviously the kind of man a person could count on—unlike that sneaky snake named Jake.

"What do you mean you're coming along?" she'd demanded a short time earlier when Jake had suddenly appeared on the sidewalk beside her as Howie drove up in a gleaming black convertible.

"I mean that Howie has decided to cohost a beach party with me to celebrate the completion of our project."

"He didn't say anything about it the other day when he asked me to the beach."

"He didn't know about the party until this morning."

Amy tried stamping her foot, but her rubber thongs made no sound against the cement. She opted instead for her sternest teacher's voice. "Jake, if you have any ideas about causing trouble, you can forget them right now. I'm going with Howie and that's all there is to it."

Jake raised an arrogant brow. "Who's trying to stop you?"

Amy pointed a finger at his broad chest. "You are," she accused.

He looked down at her, his eyes hidden behind dark glasses. "I think you're suffering from a delusion. I am an unchauvinistic, liberated man. I wouldn't dream of trying to stop you."

Amy opened her mouth again, but snapped it closed as he continued, "Besides, you won't be the only woman there, you know. Howie's invited someone along he's anxious for 'the loser,' meaning me, to meet."

Jake certainly seemed pleased about that, Amy thought. Well, she wasn't surprised. She'd known his desire for her would burn out. She was thrilled that she was right. So thrilled that she had a lump in her throat. "I never said you were a loser."

"Not in so many words, perhaps," Jake answered, his gaze fixed on the sports car.

Howie was climbing out. He smiled and waved. Amy smiled back, gritting her small, white teeth. She said in a low tone to the man at her side, "If that's what you want to believe, fine."

"Fine."

"That's just dandy."

"I think so, too," he said smoothly.

And it was, Amy decided as she stubbed her toe on a pebble hidden in the sand. She certainly didn't care what Jake thought or did. She took a few limping steps to catch back up to Howie and the rest of the group who'd met them in the Newport beach parking lot. She was here with a possible husband prospect and that was all that mattered. At least Maddie would be pleased.

She stole a surreptitious glance at the man at her side. No doubt about it, Howie was one of the handsomest men she'd ever seen. If she'd tried to conjure up a Prince Charming, he'd definitely have Howie's face and build.

To begin with, the man was at least six feet, two inches tall. His shoulders weren't quite as wide as Jake's, she decided objectively, but they came in a close second. His blond hair glinted in the sun, perfectly straight and parted to the side where it fell over his left eye in a decidedly sexy manner. His teeth were gleaming white, his lips full. His eyes were a bright blue beneath thick lashes, and they always seemed to be silently laughing at a private joke.

Howie almost seemed too good to be true. The man even had decent clothes sense—quite a shock after Shorty and Richard. For the beach party he was wearing dark blue trunks, the same color as his eyes. The trunks displayed his muscular, tanned legs to their best advantage. He wore thongs and a white cotton short-sleeved shirt opened down his chest.

She was studying that brown chest—not as much hair as Jake, she decided—when she looked up suddenly and found Howie watching her with a twinkle in his eye. A slow blush climbed up her cheeks. She glanced away, only to discover Jake's stony stare from beyond Howie. He looked at her a moment, and then without a word, turned away.

Amy's blush burned hotter. Darn it. Had both men seen her ogling Howie's chest? Something in Jake's eyes made her feel strangely guilty. Angrily rejecting the emotion, she hurried to catch up with the rest of the group as they stopped on a small rise of sand overlooking the ocean.

Sea gulls circled overhead, calling in their raucous voices. The sun hung over the ocean, casting a warm glow that sparkled on the waves rising and falling against the white sand.

Almost all of Jake's employees were there, most of them accompanied by their girlfriends or wives. Harris's wife was a plump brunette, very talkative and friendly. Shorty was proudly holding the hand of his Sue, a pretty blonde. The other half-dozen or so women were paired off with the rest of the men, with the exception of a blond woman standing close to Jake.

Howie's consolation prize to Jake, Amy deduced. With that perfect body crammed into a string bikini, she couldn't be anyone else. And Jake had had the nerve to say *her* suit was too revealing when she'd come downstairs. Ha! She could divide her suit in half and still have more than what the blonde was wearing. In fact, she had shoelaces thicker than the strings climbing the woman's buttocks. From the way he was smiling, standing around like Mr. Macho in his red trunks, Jake apparently had no problem with what the blonde's suit covered. Or didn't cover.

Reaching the summit, Amy dumped her load on the small dune. She slipped off her thongs and dug her feet into the fine sand. The top layer was burning, but underneath the fine grains were cool. She began opening chairs and setting them upright.

Amy noticed the blonde—Connie, Jake called her—was already trying to entice Jake to go for a walk along the beach. So far, though, he seemed to be resisting, holding his hands up in laughing protest, before stretching out on a blanket in the sun. Connie immediately stretched her curvy brown body next to him.

Determined to ignore Jake and his new friend, Amy slipped off her neon-green beach robe, revealing her matching swimsuit underneath.

Howie spoke over her shoulder. "Nice suit, Amy." His eyes held a masculine glint. "And if you don't mind my saying so, nice figure, too."

"I'd have to be an idiot to mind your saying something like that," Amy replied. Especially since he'd said it loud enough for the big lummox lying on the sand to hear. She'd taken extra pains with her hair and makeup as the book advised on a first date. She'd told herself it was for Howie's benefit, ignoring the tiny hope that Jake might notice and compliment her. He hadn't.

She started to shake out her towel, but Howie stopped her, producing the flannel blanket that he'd tucked under his arm. Together they spread it out, and then he held out his hand coaxingly. "Come on, Amy. Let's catch a few waves before the fire gets going."

"I don't want to go in the water, but I'll come and watch." Putting her hand in his she laughed as he pulled her down to the water's edge and in up to her knees without letting her stop. The water felt smooth and refreshing in the August heat. Amy jumped and squealed, laughing as a piece of seaweed brushed her leg.

Howie threw a casual arm around her shoulders. Leaning close, he pointed at the two stone jetties that extended into the water, perpendicular to the shore. "See those? That's where the Santa Ana River empties out. The jetties are the reason this is called The Wedge and why it's so famous for bodysurfing. The waves run along the jetty and form a wedge, perfect to ride in on." He leaned closer, coaxing, "Want to try it?"

Amy shook her head. "No, not right now. You go ahead and I'll watch awhile."

Howie jogged into the water, diving into an oncoming wave. Amy breathed a sigh of relief. It was irrational, but she'd felt uneasy when he'd put his arm around her. How stupid to feel that she was betraying Jake merely because Howie had touched her. Howie began bodysurfing, and Amy, anxious to be distracted from the problem, watched him as she waded in the shallower water.

On the beach, Jake watched sourly as Amy watched Howie cavort foolishly in the water. It wasn't enough that Amy had to wear that revealing swimsuit. It wasn't enough that she had to go out with his ex-best friend, who wasn't only tall, blonde and handsome, but was a nice guy to boot. Oh, no, as if all this wasn't enough, Amy also had the gall to enjoy herself while she was doing it.

He timed her. Amy stayed in the water almost thirty minutes watching Howie as Jake became hotter and hotter on the sand. By the time she finally came out, walked over and plopped down on the blanket, he could almost feel steam rising from his body.

So, when Connie, the blonde with the awesome figure and not-so-awesome intellect, ran her finger up his back, he didn't say a word to stop her. *Let's see how Amy handled a little jealousy.*

"So, Jakey," Connie cooed, "ready to take a little stroll?"

Jake winced. Jakey? "No, thanks," he answered shortly.

"No?" She brushed her breast against his arm.

"Not right now."

Connie sauntered off with a hopeful glance back that Jake ignored. He glanced at Amy. She was lying with her head pillowed on her arms, apparently asleep. Okay, so she handled jealousy well.

She opened her eyes and her gaze met his. "Could you throw me the suntan lotion?"

Jake began to comply with her request but changed his mind. "Here, I'll do it," he said. If anyone was going to apply lotion on Amy, it was going to be him.

He walked over and sat down next to her. Carefully, he spread the lotion on his hands, and then applied a thin layer to her back. Round and round in a circular motion he rubbed the liquid into her smooth, golden skin. His hands slid down to her waist. He glanced around. No one was watching. Stealthily, he allowed his hands to slide under the low back of Amy's bathing suit bottom.

Amy's eyes shot open but she didn't move. Surely Jake wouldn't get too blatant, would he, with everyone around? The only reason she didn't move, she told herself, was because she didn't want to cause a scene. She remained as still as possible.

Jake's hand slid along her side. Amy flinched, trying not to shiver as he passed over sensitive skin. His palm moved up along the side of her breast, barely touching the rounded curve before sliding back down again.

She felt the cool liquid followed by Jake's warm hand on the back of her calves. He moved his hand down to her ankle, then up again. Her thighs tingled as he covered as much of the area as was decently possible. He massaged along the outside of her legs, moving to her inner thigh with the same soothing, rhythmic motion.

Just when Amy felt she couldn't take another minute, he stopped. He recapped the bottle, stuck it in the sand and walked back to his blanket as Connie returned from the shoreline to lie beside him.

"Aren't you going to give me a rubdown?" Connie pouted over at Jake and unclipped the back of her swimsuit suggestively.

Amy rolled her eyes.

"Not right now, Connie," Jake answered. "How 'bout something to eat?"

"Okay, Jakey. I'm starved."

Amy gritted her teeth. She decided if she heard Connie say "Jakey" one more time, she'd get up and kick sand in the other woman's perfectly made-up face.

Howie waded out of the water, and Amy threw him a towel. He ruffled it through his hair, achieving a look of casual elegance. "Ready to eat?" he asked, cocking an eyebrow at her.

"Sure." She rose and walked with him to the fire pit.

As Howie and Amy approached, Jake jabbed a hot dog on a cooking wire with unnecessary force. His eyes narrowed at the sight of Howie's hand on Amy's elbow. *Don't lose it, don't lose it, fella,* he warned himself. *Remember: violence is never an answer.*

After all, Amy was mature enough to realize she didn't want another man; she just needed a little time. She wasn't going to be bowled over by a handsome face like Howie's. Or by blond hair—like Howie's. She wouldn't be swayed by a nice personality, a great car, an attentive manner and the other hundred and one things Howie had going for him. Amy was too smart for that.

He hoped.

Lost in his thoughts, Jake didn't notice that his hot dog had caught fire until Connie sidled over. She put her arm around his shoulders and said in a voice loud enough for everyone to hear, "Jakey, your poor little wiener has shriveled up to nothing."

"That's okay, Connie," he said in a low tone.

"Have a bite of mine," she offered.

"No, thanks."

"I insist."

Jake took a bite to keep her quiet. He was conscious of Amy watching solemnly from across the fire. Now that he thought of it, it probably hadn't been a good idea to try and make her jealous. It just gave credence to her belief that his attraction to her was temporary. Damn! If only he hadn't let the sight of Amy with Howie get to him, he wouldn't have made a mistake like that.

He had to think of a way to escape Connie and get Amy away from Howie. Thinking desperately, Jake proposed suddenly, "Let's play football."

The group gave a collective groan.

"No, I mean it," he persisted.

"I haven't finished eating yet," Shorty protested as he bit into a cupcake.

Sue gave him a patient look. "When are you ever finished, Shorty?"

Shorty protested good-naturedly while the rest of the crowd hooted. The women, with the exception of Connie, declined to play, but the men rose slowly to their feet. Rod jumped up enthusiastically, followed by Connie, and headed toward a cleared stretch of beach.

Amy and Howie hadn't moved from their chairs by the fire. Jake pinned his gaze on her. "Come on, Amy."

"I don't know how to play."

His voice deepened. "I'll show you."

As he went to join the others, Amy looked over at Howie, who'd been watching the byplay with interest. "Do you want to play football?" she asked, uncertain of his reaction.

He turned his amused blue gaze on her. "Not if my other option is getting you alone on a deserted stretch of beach."

Amy smiled a little. "I'm afraid it's not."

Howie sighed and rose lithely to his feet. "Then let's play." He pulled her to her feet, keeping her hand in his as they walked over to join the group.

"But the only women playing are Connie and me," Amy noticed, her steps lagging. "And I'm not very good at sports. I'll slow my team up."

"You'll be a star," Howie promised. "I'll help you."

Jake eyed their linked hands balefully as they came up. Expertly, he divided everyone into two groups, appointing Howie as one team captain and himself as the other. He put Amy on his team and Connie on Howie's. "No couples together," he said smoothly.

Connie's lip came down in an exaggerated pout, but to Jake's surprise, Howie made no objection. "Fine with me," he said agreeably.

Jake went back to his team with a puzzled frown on his face. Something was up with Howie but he wasn't exactly sure what it was. The man enjoyed a challenge too much to give up on Amy that easily. Especially since he knew Jake wanted her.

He shook off his uneasiness and called up the first play. Since his team had the ball, he decided to try a long pass and selected Amy as his first receiver.

He put his arm around her shoulders, looking down into her worried face. "Now remember. When I say 'hike' you head out toward the volleyball courts. Don't look back. Just keep running and I'll throw the ball. Try to catch it and run for a touchdown."

"Okay," Amy said unenthusiastically.

He slapped her on the bottom. "Let's have some pep!"

"Gotcha!" she said louder, giving him a sour look.

Both sides lined up. Jake called out a series of numbers and went back for a long throw. Connie tried to tackle him, but he easily sidestepped her and threw the ball as hard as he could.

It was then he realized he'd made a tactical error.

Howie was downfield with Amy. The blond man easily could have deflected the ball away from her or caught it for an interception. Instead, he let Amy catch it. She grinned and began running. Sprinting, Howie quickly reached her and swept her up. He carried her back to the scrimmage line where he gently dropped her in the sand. Helping her to her feet again, he made a big production of brushing her off.

Jake scowled.

On the next play, he made sure he threw the ball to someone else. It didn't matter. Howie still tackled Amy.

If he wanted to maintain his nonviolent status, Jake decided he'd better do something fast. He called time-out and announced the team captains would be trading teams. Connie smiled. The men exchanged surprised glances, but no one, not even Shorty, protested.

They assembled into their huddles again. This time Howie's team had the ball. Howie feinted and threw to Amy. Before Jake could get to her, though, Rod had tackled her. Howie, with a mischievous glance at Jake's set face, continued to throw only to Amy.

The next play, Shorty caught her.

The following one, a man Jake didn't even know put his arms around her slim waist and brought her to the ground.

While Connie retied her neck strap by the scrimmage line, the men met in their defensive huddle for the last play. Jake was thoroughly frustrated. He gave each man a threatening glare. "The next one who touches Amy," he growled, "is going to be eating sand."

"What did you say, boss?" Shorty asked.

"I said," Jake replied through gritted teeth, "that the next person to tackle Amy is going to be eating sand. Lots of dirty, damp sand."

This time no one asked for clarification. Satisfied that he'd made his point, Jake led his team back to the line drawn on the beach.

Howie called the plays and again Amy was thrown the ball. She bumped into Shorty, who quickly stepped aside. She dashed past Rod, who didn't lift a hand to stop her.

"Amy, wait! You're going the wrong way!" Howie called frantically.

Confused, Amy spun around and started back. Jake's team almost appeared to be covering for her as they rushed to get out of her way.

Jake tried to make his way through the mob to tackle her himself, but stumbled as he felt something clinging to his ankle. He looked down. Connie was lying full length in the sand holding on to him. "Gotcha!" she said with a wide grin.

Jake rolled his eyes heavenward as Amy spiked the ball at the other end of the field.

Chapter Thirteen

The setting, Amy decided three hours later, was perfect for seduction.

A bright full moon lit the starry sky, highlighting foamy white waves in the darkness. The sea breeze brushing her face left a salty mist on her lips. Most important, the man—the *handsome* man sitting next to her—was eligible, intelligent and successful. Yes, according to the book, everything was just right.

Why then did it all feel so wrong?

Amy looked over at Howie's shadowy figure. He absently sifted sand through his fingers as he stared out at the ocean. The few twinges of uneasiness she'd felt with him earlier had faded during the physical exertion of playing football. So after the game, when the rest of the group collapsed laughing around the fire and he'd asked her to take a walk on the beach, she hadn't hesitated to agree.

The uneasiness returned as they strolled farther and farther, until the fire was only a small speck in the distance. It escalated when he'd casually slung a heavy arm around her shoulders as they walked, and she'd caught the interested masculine gleam in his eyes. By the time Howie pulled her down to sit on the sand beneath the station, she felt a clamor of alarm that she could no longer ignore.

He looked at her, and Amy could see his white teeth gleaming in the darkness as he moved closer. Bending forward to examine a broken bit of shell in the sand provided the perfect excuse to escape his encircling arm.

Somehow, when she'd imagined searching for Mr. Right, she'd pictured long serious conversations with the prospective husbands, similar to job interviews. She hadn't expected a candidate who'd want to move past the talking and on to what the book called "the physical compatibility" test, more commonly known as the first kiss, quite so fast. She asked abruptly, "Do you like children, Howie?"

The book didn't advise asking that question on a first date, Amy knew. At this point, she didn't care. If the man was going to make a move on her, if she was going to seriously consider him as a husband, she wanted to find out ahead of time whether or not he fit her specifications.

In the moonlight she could see the frown that pulled his blond, perfectly shaped eyebrows down over his eyes. "Children?" His arm dropped. "You don't have any children, do you?"

"No," she admitted. He relaxed a little. He turned toward her again, and Amy brought her knees up to her chest, hugging them tightly. The night was turning cool; she should have put on more than just her beach robe over her suit. She rested her chin on her knees as she dug her toes—her Flintstone toes—into the warm sand beneath the cooling top layer.

Howie leaned a little closer, and she said brightly, "But I want kids someday."

"So do I." His white smile gleamed in the dark. "Someday."

"Lots of kids," Amy persisted.

His smile widened. "Sounds great."

Okay, so he'd passed that question, Amy thought, disgruntled. That didn't mean he'd pass them all. She scooted over the tiniest bit as Howie lounged closer on one elbow. "By the way, Jake said you were in the same class in college," she mentioned.

"I was three years behind him, but since we were in related fields, we had a few classes together." Howie edged a little closer.

Amy frowned, as she calculated his age. She sighed. Okay, so he'd passed that specification, too. Well, now that she thought about it, age wasn't really important. She'd hit him with the big one. "Have you ever been married?"

"No." Howie put his arm around her waist.

"I suppose you don't believe in marriage, having such a demanding career and everything," she said hurriedly. His smooth palm gently turned her face toward him. Howie's fingertips felt soft compared to Jake's callused ones, she noticed, then quickly pushed the thought aside as he loomed closer.

He said in his sexy baritone, "Marriage is more important than any career, in my opinion. I hope to have a relationship like my parents—equal partners in all they did." His breath, smelling faintly of mint, flowed across her cheek. "I'm just waiting for the right woman."

As he tried to kiss her, Amy put up her hands, pushing against his chest and turning her face to the side. He immediately dropped his arms from around her.

They moved apart, both sitting up now. Howie's calm voice sounded out of the darkness. "So, there is something going on between you and Jake."

"No!"

"Well, if it's not that, what is it? Am I coming on too strong? Not strong enough?"

"It's nothing like that, it's just..." Amy felt miserable. What could she say? That she couldn't bear to kiss him? That Howie just didn't arouse any of the whirling desire that Jake stirred without effort? But wasn't that what she wanted? Not to be blinded by lust?

Howie put his arm around her and gave her a brotherly hug. "I'm sorry, Amy. I didn't mean to push you."

Darn, the man *was* too perfect, Amy thought. She suspected Howie came as close to Mr. Right as anyone could.

She still didn't want him to kiss her.

That realization led Amy to another: Mr. Right or not, if she didn't desire Howie, there was no way she could be intimate with him. And if she *did* desire him, then he wasn't Mr. Right because lust didn't last.

This was a dilemma she hadn't considered. She slapped savagely at the grains of sand clinging to her legs. What a time to realize her plan had a major flaw with Howie sitting beside her.

She searched for something to say to end the thickening silence. Not one intelligent remark came to mind. She stifled a groan. What an awkward situation. What could be worse?

Jake's voice growled out of the darkness behind them. "So *this* is where you two are."

Amy groaned aloud this time. Okay, so this was worse. She looked at Jake over her shoulder. "What are you doing here?" she demanded.

He took a threatening step toward Howie. "I'm stopping you from doing something you *might* regret, and Howie from something he will *definitely* regret." His fists clenched at his sides, he stared at the other man menacingly.

"Hello, Jake." To Amy, Howie sounded less worried than resigned. He rose gracefully to his feet, brushing at the sand on his shorts, before extending a hand to help her rise.

Accepting it, she jumped up and stepped between the two men. Hands on hips, she faced Jake. "This is between Howie and me," she said firmly. "You stay out of it."

"No," Jake answered bluntly. Reaching out, he shackled her wrist with his hand, and pulled her to his side. "You've got that wrong. This is between you and *me*, not Howie. He's just a fun-loving, not-so-innocent bystander who's gotten in the way, and who," he continued deliberately, "better get out of the way. Fast."

Before Amy could voice the words burning on her tongue, Howie intervened, holding his hands up in surrender. "I'm out of here, pal." He looked at Amy regretfully. "I just had to see what was making you act so crazy."

"Yeah, I could see you were enjoying yourself. Unless you want to see me really let go, I suggest you disappear immediately. And take Connie with you," Jake added as an afterthought.

"Sure thing. See you around, Amy," Howie said as he brushed past them.

Amy watched him stride toward the fire pit in the distance.

Thoughts of Howie fled as Jake tugged on her wrist. Startled, she looked up as he began walking toward the shoreline, pulling her after him.

"Where are you going?" She jerked at her wrist but his grip didn't loosen. He continued to march to the water. "What are you doing? The water's too cold. I don't want to get wet."

"Amy, I've decided you don't know what you want. So from now on, we'll do things my way."

"Jake! Wait a minute. We need to talk." He kept on going. She tried to pry his fingers away, but his grip only tightened, bringing her closer and closer to the water. She leaned back, digging her heels in the now-damp sand. When that didn't work, she sat down.

Pausing, Jake released her. Amy watched warily as he stripped off his black sweatshirt and threw it down. His black T-shirt followed. Wearing only his trunks, his broad figure was a dark silhouette against the backdrop of the white, roaring waves.

He bent. She gave a startled squeak as he picked her up in his arms and carried her toward the ocean. Inexplicably frightened, Amy struggled harder as he waded into the water. The first wave broke against Jake's calves. She stopped fighting to get down and threw her arms around his muscled neck, arching up to try and stay out of the cold water.

She looked up at his face. His mouth was a straight line cutting across the stony planes of his cheeks and chin. His eyes glittered angrily down at her. Somehow hurt by his expression, Amy swallowed. "Jake, stop this. You're scaring me."

He halted thigh-deep in the surging water. Another wave crashed against them, shooting cold spray against Amy's legs and back and sprinkling Jake's face with glistening drops. His arms tightened under her knees and shoulders as he said fiercely, "I'm scaring you? What do you think you did to me going off with Howie like that?"

"I wasn't trying to upset you. I was just trying to give my plan a chance. To find out—"

"I don't want to hear this."

"If Howie was Mr. Right," she continued unheedingly.

His arms tightened, crushing her against his warm chest. "For you, *I* am Mr. Right. The search is *over*, Amy."

She shook her head, feeling miserable and confused. Couldn't he see it would never work? "But, Jake, don't you understand—"

"No more stupid excuses. After seeing you with Howie, I'm not in the mood to listen."

"But, Jake—"

"Don't argue with me."

"But—"

He released her, and Amy gasped in the excruciating second before she dropped. Then tingling cold darkness closed around her. Salty water filled her mouth and nose while something slimy wrapped around her arm. She flailed desperately, trying to stand up in the swirling sea.

Strong arms came around her, lifting her. Now the air felt chilly and the water warm. Sputtering, Amy flung an arm around Jake's solid neck, while with her other hand she clawed at the seaweed clinging to her chest. Shuddering with revulsion, she flung the brown vine into a receding wave.

Her hair was plastered flatly to her skull. One annoying, sticky strand hung down over her eyes. She pushed it back, then tilted her head to drain the water from her ears.

Jake's voice sounded muffled to her as he said, "That's one way to shut you up. Do you have anything you want to add?"

She coughed and spit out the saltwater burning her throat. "I am going to kill you," she said, when she was finally able to speak coherently.

Jake waded back to the shore. "No, you won't. Because chances are I'll kill you first if we don't get this straight."

He carried her up the dune to where his shirts created a black patch on the sand and set her on her feet. Picking up his T-shirt, he stroked off the water running down her face, arms and legs before drying himself. He rubbed the shirt over his hair. He toweled hers with it also before dropping it in the sand.

Amy stood quietly, feeling limp as he removed her soggy beach robe. She was wet. She was cold. Most of all, she was confused. She stiffened as, before she could protest, Jake suddenly stripped off her wet suit top.

She glanced down. Her white breasts glowed, appearing almost fluorescent in the night, speckled with dark bits of shell and sand. Her nipples puckered tightly. Her hands flew up to cover them, but Jake was already tugging his sweatshirt over her head and pulling her arms through the long sleeves. The soft cotton fell down to her thighs. She crossed her arms, huddling in its warmth.

He pulled her into his arms, and she rested her cheek against his chest. She'd kill him later. Right now, his arms were too comforting to resist.

He spoke above her head. "Amy, you have to give up this stupid scheme."

She shook her head, wearily. "It's not a stupid scheme. When people follow their hearts instead of their heads, they get hurt. My mother got hurt, so did my father. They were both lonely all during their marriage, and so was I."

She lifted her hand and absently brushed sand off his muscular arm. "My father didn't make the same mistake with his second wife. He chose her calmly and unemotionally, and they are perfectly content. I'm going to do the same. I don't want to be alone anymore. I want a relationship that will last."

Jake caught her hand in his and carried it up to his mouth. He pressed his lips to her salty palm. "I'm sorry your parents were unhappy, that you were unhappy. But it wouldn't have to be the same for us. The important thing is that I want you and you want me. When are you going to admit that?" He kissed her slender fingers.

Amy pulled her hand away. "Don't you understand what I'm telling you? What people want isn't always good for them."

"It will be good." Jake hugged her, his voice rumbling by her ear. "What we have is too special, too important, to just ignore. I want you more than I've ever wanted anyone in my life."

"But you've known me for ten long years. Don't you find it strange that you've only noticed me as a woman now?"

"I don't think it's strange." He gently brushed her damp hair back from her wide brow. Her eyes glistened up at him, looking almost black in her pale face. He said softly, "Before, age was a gap between us. You were a kid and I was an adult. Maddie would have shot me if I'd ever shown an interest in you." He gave a rueful chuckle. "For all I know, she might shoot me even now."

He gripped her shoulders, holding her tightly. "But you've always been special to me. You were like family, but even more, you were my friend. You made me laugh, you made me angry, you made me feel—you still make me feel—emotions I've never felt with anyone else."

He cradled her face, tilting it up to his as he whispered huskily, "No one else will do, Amy. It's only you I need."

Amy shut her eyes. His words touched her. All her life it seemed she'd been waiting to belong to someone. Attaching herself to Maddie and Jake had been a desperate attempt to share the sense of family, the sense of love, woven so deeply between them. The love her own family lacked.

Jake wasn't offering love, but passion could be a potent substitute. Even though it wouldn't last, couldn't last. But if she gave in to desire, what would she do once it was over? She'd have lost his friendship—and possibly Maddie's. She'd be more alone than she was even now.

She could feel Jake's lips roving over her cheeks and eyelids, along her temple and then down, seeking her mouth. Was she being a coward to resist? Wouldn't it be better to enjoy the desire between them—no matter how fleeting—than wonder for the rest of her life how making love with Jake would feel?

Her heart clenched at the thought. Because the truth was, she loved him. He wasn't right for her. He wasn't the man who could give her forever. But forever was a long way off when she was here with him now.

Reaching a decision, she linked her arms around his neck. His breath caught. Slowly he exhaled as he drew her closer. He lowered his head and outlined the curves of her lips with the tip of his tongue, before parting her mouth with his own.

Amy moaned. The warm security she always felt with Jake dissolved under more urgent emotions; emotions Jake was coaxing forth with his hungry mouth and sure touch. Her peaked nipples pushed against his hard chest. Before she was completely aware of the small distraction, Jake's hand covered them, massaging first one breast then the other to aching fullness.

Without lifting his mouth from hers, he walked her backward toward the lifeguard station, sinking into the shadows beneath it. He stretched out in the sand, and drew her down with him, pillowing her head on the hard muscles of his arm.

Lifting his head, he looked down at her in the soft shadows. The waves roared toward the beach in time with the rising and falling of her chest beneath his shirt. He pulled the material up over her flat stomach. Carefully, he bared her breasts, brushing at the grains embedded in her soft flesh.

Amy opened her eyes and then quickly closed them again, shifting under his hands. It was too much. Too much piercing pleasure.

Her stomach muscles clenched and her head fell back when he covered her breast with his mouth, sucking slowly on her nipple. When he'd tightened the tension to an almost unbearable degree, he moved to her other one, covering the first breast gently with his callused palm.

Amy's hands slid up to his arms, skimming off the sand coating his smooth skin. There was no give in those arms, not a pinchable inch of fat anywhere on Jake's hard body. Testing her discovery, her palms roved up his wide shoulders and down over the coarse hair sprinkled on his chest. She stroked along his stomach to his navel, hesitated, and moved her hand back up around his neck.

Jake released the breath he'd been holding. Lying back, he shifted her on top of him. With one hand on her bottom, he nestled her against the portion of his anatomy that ached the most. He caressed her slender back, running his hand down her spine, and sliding under her damp suit. Her mouth lowered to his as he slowly stroked the cool curve of her buttocks. He wanted to touch her there, and there.

Amy moaned. Voices sounded in the distance, and Jake suddenly pulled away. Quickly, he sat up, carrying her with him. He settled her in his lap, kissed her damp curls and then rested his chin on top of her head. "We need to get home, Amy. Fast."

She nodded, and he rewarded her with a hug. For a moment he cuddled her, enjoying the cool breeze, the pounding surf, the woman in his arms. It was beautiful. It was a night they'd always remember. Together.

Amy stirred in his arms, and he shifted, snuggling her closer. Happiness too deep to be contained welled up in his chest. Bending, he whispered in her ear, "Before we leave, I need to know. How soon are you going to marry me?"

He waited expectantly for her answer. And waited. By the time the silence had stretched to a minute, he knew he wasn't going to get the answer he wanted.

Through the shadows, he could see the slight frown that drew her brows together, and for the first time, she pulled away a little. Jake's muscles clenched. *Please, God, not again.*

"Married?" Her voice sounded hesitant. "You don't want to get married." She awkwardly climbed off him. Under his dispassionate gaze, she yanked his shirt down to cover her breasts.

His jaw clenched. "Yes, Amy, I do want to get married. Don't you?"

"Yes, but not . . ." She stopped, confused.

"But not to me," Jake finished flatly. Rage engulfed him. Slowly, he stood up, not once taking his gaze off her.

Amy rose, too, brushing at the sand covering her arms. "You don't understand, Jake," she said softly.

He laughed harshly. "Yes, I do. I finally do. You're a hypocrite and a coward. You talk about commitment, yet you aren't prepared to make a commitment yourself. At least not with me. You were only using me as a temporary release until you moved on to someone better, someone who fulfills the fantasy you've been creating."

She slowly shook her head.

He ignored the movement, his eyes hard in the moonlight. "I never expected that from you, Amy.

Which shows what a fool I am. Because I doubt you'll ever grow up and face reality." Turning, he began walking away, into the darkness. His voice drifted back to where she stood. "We'd better get going. The party's over."

Chapter Fourteen

"Happy birthday, darling. And welcome home."

Amy looked up from her seat on Maddie's white couch. Maddie halted in the doorway, her face glowing above a candlelit cake. The turquoise dress she wore was a slash of color in the white room. The dress complemented the light tan she'd received on her trip. On her left hand, a diamond engagement ring sparkled almost as brightly as her silver-gray eyes.

Smiling, she walked into the room and lowered the cake onto the glass coffee table in front of Amy. "Now make a wish, dear, and blow them out."

Amy stared down at the cake. It was flat on one side and oddly puffy on the other. Maddie had frosted it too soon. The pink icing had melted into a thin layer on top before running over the sides. Between the flickering candles, Maddie had spelled out with chocolate chips, "Hap. Bir. Amy."

"I ran out of chips," Maddie explained, setting silver forks and china plates next to the cake. She sat down by Amy and picked up the silver serving knife. "You haven't made your wish, dear," she reminded gently.

Amy swallowed the tears building in her throat. Make a wish. She closed her eyes and, despite her best intentions, visualized Jake's face. His silvery eyes, teasing grin, rugged chin. She opened her eyes quickly and Maddie's eyes met hers.

"What's wrong, darling?" The older woman's voice was low, her eyes understanding as she patted Amy's hand as it rested on the table. "What did my grandson do to hurt you so?"

Amy forced a smile. She smoothed down her skirt in an attempt to avoid the other woman's gaze. "He didn't do anything, Maddie," she answered lightly. Except ask me to marry him—without loving me. "I wanted to start getting my apartment ready. School is opening in a week, and Jake is so busy. It was past time that I got out of his way." And came back to reality.

Maddie's expression told Amy she didn't believe a word, but other than raising a skeptical eyebrow, she didn't pursue the issue. "Blow out your candles."

Amy leaned over and blew, only extinguishing half. It didn't matter. Her wish was impossible, anyway.

Maddie removed the candles, then picked up the knife. "Well, darling. How did your plan go?"

Amy busied herself putting out the plates. "I discovered my plan wasn't practical in the cold light of reason. It had a major flaw. If I don't love a man, then I can't bring myself to make love with him. And if I do, then I don't want him to be tricked into marriage.''

Maddie looked amused. Her silver eyes—Jake's eyes—crinkled with amusement. "Darling, do you really believe you can trick a man into marriage?''

Amy looked at her. "The book claims—''

Maddie dismissed the book with a wave of her slender white hand, her diamond sparkling with the movement. "The book is merely a tool, at best, to give women the confidence to go after what they want.'' Her mouth quirked wryly. "Believe me, darling, women have been doing *that* before Dr. Potocki was even born. There's nothing in that book that can make a man marry you who doesn't want to.''

"You don't understand.'' Abstractedly, Amy accepted the plate of cake Maddie put in her hand. "The book gives methods—''

"Methods, smethods.'' Maddie held out a fork.

Amy took it and set it down. "But, Maddie, I thought you believed in the book. Isn't that how you attracted George? You said two men were vying for your attention the whole trip.''

"They were.'' Maddie delicately picked a chip off her cake with her fork, and lifted it to her mouth. "George wasn't. He's too arrogant. He saw me, decided he wanted me, and while my other two suitors were fighting over a shuffleboard game, he took me off dancing.'' She ate another chip. "It was so romantic, darling. He's really very macho. Eat some cake.''

Amy cut off a piece, lifted it to her mouth, then lowered it suddenly. "George fit your specifications, didn't he?''

"He certainly did. He loves me.''

"Is that enough, Maddie?" Amy bit her lower lip. "How do you know it will last if you don't have anything in common?"

Maddie selected another tiny chocolate chip. "It might not, unless we nurture it. Eat some cake, dear." Amy obediently took a small bite. "The way you need to nurture Jake's love for you," Maddie continued.

Amy's eyes widened as she considered Maddie's words. As soon as she could speak, she choked out, "What makes you think Jake loves me?"

Maddie looked at her with amused indulgence. "Darling, Jake fell in love the moment he met you. Oh, he didn't realize it—after all, my grandson is no cradle snatcher—but whether he knows it or not, all these years he's been waiting for you to grow up."

Amy shook her head in bewilderment. "Maddie, that can't be true. Why, he always looked on me as an annoyance."

"Annoyance!" Maddie laughed. "Darling, Jake was more anxious to see you on his visits than he was me. How many young men in their twenties would let a teenager tag after them?"

"But—"

"Haven't you noticed how Jake bristled like a dog with a favorite bone whenever any young man came near you?"

"But—"

"My goodness! He even ate that dreadful pie you made, just so he wouldn't hurt your feelings."

"But—"

"Darling, when are you going to let go of old fears to make room to love him back?"

Amy's eyes burned. "I already love him. But Maddie, he only asked me to marry him because I'd tricked him with the book."

Maddie patted her on the shoulder. "Darling, if he asked you to marry him, then of course he loves you."

"Then why didn't he say so?"

"Probably because he's a big idiot." Maddie picked up her plate again. "Most men are when it comes to love. They feel it. They just don't know they feel it until we coax it out of them. Jake is worst than most. He thinks he's so tough, but I'm afraid my grandson is a pussycat at heart."

"I know." Pulling a tissue from her purse, Amy blew her nose. Jake was soft-hearted. He treated his employees like family. He could have retired Rosie years ago, but the thought would never occur to him as long as she wanted to keep working. He couldn't say "no" to anyone in trouble. Even though he had thought Amy's husband-hunt was stupid, he'd still agreed to help her. And he hated to refuse Maddie anything. "He loves you a lot," Amy said.

Maddie smiled. "I think he does, too, dear. Although the property alone is worth a small fortune now, he's never even mentioned remodeling the beach house because he knows I love it the way it is."

So did Amy. She looked down at the cake on the platter. It was as pitiful as one Jake would have made. "Oh, Maddie. I miss him so much. I wish I could believe you're right—that he loves me and it will last. I just don't want to end up with a marriage like my parents'."

Maddie's gaze met hers. "Darling, life doesn't give us any guarantees. Are you happier now, away from Jake, than you would be with him?"

"No," Amy admitted. "I've been miserable."

Maddie smiled sadly. "Love isn't something you can turn off and on at will. Jake's grandfather may no longer be here with me, but I'll never stop loving him, even now that I love George."

Her eyes held a faraway look. "With Jake's grandfather I hurt when I was away from him, and yes, darling, sometimes I hurt when I was with him. He exasperated and delighted me. He fulfilled my wildest fantasies, and at other times, he disappointed me more than anyone on this earth. But none of this affected my love for him or his love for me, darling. True love is the only thing in this world you can definitely count on."

Amy clenched her tissue in her hand. Maddie was right. It wasn't passion that had destroyed her parents' marriage; their marriage had crumbled because there was no love to sustain it. If only Maddie was right about Jake...

She looked over at the other woman. "Maddie, even if he did love me, he doesn't anymore. I've blown it with him."

Maddie's laughter filled the room. Standing, she picked up the remains of the cake and piled it on the tray. "Darling, if he can forgive you for five long days of diarrhea, then he can forgive you for anything." Chuckling softly, she left the room.

Amy sat on the white couch, thinking. Would he forgive her? She'd never seen him look as cold and remote as he had that last night at the beach. He'd hardly spoken to her the next day before she left. Could she take the chance he'd reject her again?

Amy straightened. Hadn't she learned anything this summer? Jake was the most important thing in her life. What could she do but go after him? She lifted her chin with determination. He would forgive her. He had to.

Somehow she'd find a way.

Chapter Fifteen

"It's hopeless."

"It can't be."

"I tell you, it's hopeless," Amy said firmly.

She picked up one of the biscuits the teenage boy in front of her was holding on a platter. She dropped it on her desk. The biscuit bounced, hard as a rock.

Amy shook her head. "You know in order to get a passing grade, you have to be able to eat your project, Paul. Your team will have to start over."

"But I can eat it, Miss Larkin. Honest."

"Don't even try it." Amy removed the platter from his hands. "Now get back to your group and make sure the others have finished cleaning up. I'll be by to grade you."

Grumbling loudly, the student left.

Amy lifted a corner of the white apron covering her blue cotton dress and dabbed at the perspiration on her temples. The home economics classroom was hot, partly from the heat of eight ovens, and partly by the energy emitted by twenty-five male students. "Next!" she called.

A boy with liquid brown eyes and a gold earring sauntered over. Amy studied the rolls he held out for her inspection. "Those look pretty good, José."

She chose one of the small brown biscuits, took a bite and chewed thoughtfully. She swallowed and smiled at him. "They taste great, too. If you've cleaned up your work area properly, your group gets an A and the honor of giving your biscuits to the principal."

José scowled, flinging back his dark hair. "Hey, man, we don't want to give them to no prin-ci-pal, Miss Larkin. I tell you, the dude's fat enough already. Why can't we eat them?"

"Eat them yourselves if you want, but no more insulting remarks about Mr. Peters."

"But he is, I tell you. Everybody knows—you can't miss it. O-be-si-ty city."

Amy opened the black notebook sitting off to one side of her desk. "You've just earned half an hour detention after school," she said, jotting down his name. When he opened his mouth to protest, she pointed the pencil at him warningly. "One more word on the subject and you'll be visiting the principal personally. Get back to work before you talk yourself into bigger trouble."

She stood up as José stamped off. Skirting small groups of students, she walked past each of the kitchen areas, monitoring progress.

At the last cubicle, a boy, taller than herself, stood with his arms folded. With a bored expression on his acne-mottled face, he watched while the other members of his group bustled around, measuring and preparing ingredients.

"Randall? Why aren't you helping?" Amy asked him.

He shrugged his thin shoulders. "I'm the waiter again."

"Why aren't you cooking?"

"Ah, Miss Larkin. I don't want to. Real men don't cook."

"Yes, they do," Amy responded.

"No, they don't."

"Yes, they do," said a deep voice behind her. Amy tensed, then slowly turned around. It was Jake.

She stood motionless a moment, her nerves humming at the sight of him. He looked bigger, broader, than she remembered as he towered above the seventh graders. Her gaze moved slowly over him. His hair was longer, curling over his collar. His plaid flannel shirt hung outside his denim jeans, and his work boots, for once, were free of mud.

Her eyes lifted to his face. He looked leaner, older somehow, the tiny lines by his eyes more deeply etched. He smiled, but his gray eyes were serious as he studied her in return. "How are you, Amy?"

"Fine." Her voice sounded husky. Nervously, she cleared her throat. During the past few weeks, she'd imagined what she'd say to him a thousand times. Now she couldn't think of anything to add to that one small word.

The silence stretching between them was broken by a demanding voice. "I tell you, I need to talk to Miss Larkin," José said, as he elbowed his way between his fellow students to stare at Jake challengingly. "Hey, man. Who are you?"

"I'm the new vice principal," Jake said coolly. "I need to talk to Miss Larkin, too. I want an immediate report from her on the troublemakers in this class." He shot the boy a significant glance.

José's eyes widened. He stepped back, holding up his hands. "Hey, man. No problem." He moved back another step, then turned and disappeared into the group.

The other students within listening distance dispersed also. Grasping Amy's elbow, Jake steered her toward the hall. "We'd better escape while we still can. Can you leave these hellions alone while we talk in the hall?"

Amy nodded, her elbow tingling from the touch of his fingers. "Yes, of course. They all have jobs to do, and—" she raised her voice to be heard above the low hum of the students' chatter "—they had better get them done, or they'll all face detention."

They stepped out into the hall, and Jake shut the windowed door firmly behind them. He turned and met her eyes. "Rosie gave me your message this morning."

"Oh. I didn't expect you here so soon."

He shrugged. "I thought I'd better drive up right away. She said you needed to see me." He looked at her, his muscles tensing. His gray eyes sharpened. "Is there something wrong with Maddie that you wanted to tell me in person?"

"Oh, no. Nothing like that." Nervously, Amy touched her hair. It was a mess, she just knew it. And she probably didn't have a bit of lipstick left on her lips. "It's I. I mean, me." She took a deep breath and tried again. "I have a problem."

Jake nodded. Leaning back against the pea-green wall, he folded his arms in front of his chest. "What is it?"

Amy swallowed, pushing her hand into her apron pocket. Her fingers closed around the folded sheet of paper she'd carried like a talisman for the past week. "I need your help."

He shrugged. "You've got it. So what's wrong?"

Everything. The word hovered on Amy's tongue, but she bit it back. She'd known this was going to be hard; she just hadn't realized exactly how hard. How could she reach a man who had retired behind an emotional wall of stone?

Nothing was going as she'd hoped. She wanted him to smile at her, to look at her with his eyes filled with smoky desire that she'd shied away from seeing before.

It was the hope Maddie was right, that Jake *did* love her, that had given her the courage to contact him. Now, under the indifference in his expression, that faint hope, along with her resolution, was fading fast.

Still, she had to try. What did she have to lose? Besides, never again would she run away from her fears.

She pulled the crumpled sheet out of her pocket and clutched it in her hand. Her eyes met his shuttered ones. "I'm afraid I made a mistake before."

"A mistake?"

"Yes. I gave you the wrong list of specifications. Here's my new version." Her fingers trembled slightly as she held out the folded sheet.

Jake looked down at the paper. The tiny flare of joy that had burned for a moment when she said she'd made a mistake was doused. He'd hoped, how he'd hoped, that somehow Amy had changed her mind about marrying him. During the three-hour drive, one thought had tumbled over and over in his mind. She'd called for him. In a time of trouble, he was the one she had turned to. Surely, they could build on that.

Because he wasn't sure he could live without her, not after having had her close. The beach house was shadowy and bleak, each room holding echoes of Amy's laughter. His job, the work that he'd found so fulfilling, had simply become an activity to help fill the days. He didn't even watch baseball anymore. Nothing was the same without her.

He'd missed her every day, every hour, every second since she'd been gone. And he'd prayed that she was missing him, too.

Well, once again, he was wrong. Instead of forgetting about her husband hunt, Amy planned to continue it. By asking for his help, she was obviously trying to put their relationship back where they'd started. Just friends. Could he live with that when every part of him clamored for more?

He didn't want to.

But could he live without her in his life at all?

No.

Slowly, Jake reached out and took Amy's list. Friendship, if it was all he could get, would have to do. He couldn't bear to lose her completely.

A dull ache spreading in his chest, he carefully unfolded the crumpled sheet. Taking a deep breath, he looked down at Amy's slanted handwriting.

Age 30: We'll grow old together.

His brows knit slightly. So, she'd upped her age request.

He read the next line. *A man who cares about those around him, such as his grandmother, his employees and especially his friends.*

Jake's muscles clenched. He frowned a little, his gaze moving lower. *A man who is protective; a man who in this liberated world isn't afraid to be a man.*

Jake felt his heart was locked in his throat. Afraid to hope, even more afraid not to, he read on. *A man who makes me believe that passion can last forever.*

He looked up. Amy smiled uncertainly, her lips trembling.

His eyes dropped to the final item on the paper. *A man who is everything a man should be, the only man for me—Jake Joseph Weston.*

He studied the words, absorbing them in his mind, his heart. Slowly he lifted his eyes to meet Amy's shimmering blue gaze. "Do you mean it, Amy? Am I the man you've been looking for?" he said, quietly.

"Oh, Jake." Tears burning in her eyes, she took a step toward him. "I've never meant anything more."

He wrapped his arms fiercely around her. Jake lifted her off her feet, burying his face in her neck, as he turned in a slow circle, squeezing her tightly. Setting her down, he brushed back her hair. "Oh, babe."

His lips found hers. He trailed kisses over her temple, cheek and eyes, only to return to her mouth again and again.

He pressed his cheek to hers. "Amy. How I've missed you, sweetheart."

Her arms around his neck, she stood on tiptoe to hug him tightly. "Oh, Jake. I've missed you, too. Can you ever forgive me? I didn't mean to hurt you that day on the beach, it was just—"

His palm covered her mouth gently. "That day I said things that I shouldn't have. I told you to grow up and face reality, yet I hadn't faced it myself."

His voice deepened as his serious eyes looked into hers. "Because I love you, Amy. More than you'll ever know. And I should have told you so."

Amy's eyes darkened. "Jake, I love you, too."

He looked at her steadily. "And you're no longer afraid our passion will burn itself out?"

She reached up to cradle his stubborn jaw. "I've learned something about passion," she said.

"You have?"

She nodded solemnly, trying to contain the smile that threatened to emerge any moment. "Yes. I've learned that the fire of passion will last as long as you—" she kissed his neck, his chin, his lean cheeks, "—keep stoking it."

"I'll agree to that." His mouth covered hers.

"Hey, guys. Miss Larkin is making out with the prin-ci-pal!" José informed the students behind him as he peeked out of a corner of the windowed door.

"The fat principal?"

"Oh, gross, man. Of course not. Miss Larkin wouldn't kiss just an-y-bo-dy. Ooeee—this guy can really *cook*."

* * * * *